THE FIVE AND CAVALIER'S TREASURE

THE FIVE are Julian, Dick,
George (Georgina by rights), Anne and
Timmy the dog.

A summer holiday with their friends Tinker
and Mischief the monkey gives the Five
a chance to explore an area a short
distance from Kirrin Cottage. And it's not
long before they discover buried treasure –
which guarantees an exciting time for
everyone!

Cover illustration by Peter Mennim

The Five and the Cavalier's Treasure

Claude Voilier
translated by Anthea Bell

Hodder
Children's
Books

a division of Hodder Headline plc

British Library Cataloguing in Publication Data

Voilier, Claude
The Five And The Cavalier's Treasure
I. Title   II. La fortune sourit
843.914 [J]   PZ7
ISBN 0 340 60327 5

Typeset by Hewer Text Composition Services, Edinburgh
Printed and bound in Great Britain by
Cox & Wyman Ltd, Reading, Berkshire

Hodder Children's Books
a division of Hodder Headline plc
338 Euston Road
London NW1 3BH

Contents

— 1 —

Off to Rose Cottage

'Wake up, George! Are you asleep on your feet, or what?' asked Dick.

The four Kirrin cousins had just got off their bicycles, and were standing by the roadside, at the garden gate of a cottage. George had been staring straight ahead of her, absent-mindedly patting her dog Timmy. Now she turned to Dick.

'Of course I'm not asleep!' she said indignantly. 'I'm thinking, that's all!'

She and Dick were eleven years old. They both had dark, curly, short hair, and looked rather like each other. Dick couldn't help laughing.

'I say, you two, did you hear that?' he asked his brother and sister, Julian and Anne. 'George's mind is ticking over! George is actually thinking! What marvellous idea will our brilliant cousin's superbrain come up with next?'

'Oh, don't be such an ass, Dick!' said Julian,

smiling. 'If you two are going to *start* the summer holidays by squabbling, what *will* you be like by the end of them?'

Julian was thirteen, and he was the eldest of the children. He was very sensible for his age. He didn't look much like his brother Dick – he was tall, and had fair hair. So did their little sister Anne.

George's three cousins nearly always spent their holidays with her – and of course with Timmy her dog too. Timmy went everywhere with George, whose real name was Georgina. This summer the children had been going to stay at Kirrin Cottage as usual. George lived there with her parents, Uncle Quentin and Aunt Fanny – the house was by the seaside and near Kirrin village. But then, unfortunately, something unexpected had happened, and that meant a change of plan for the four cousins.

George was already opening her mouth to answer Dick back, but Anne got in first, in her soft little voice.

'What were you thinking about, George? Tell us, please do!'

'Oh,' said George, rather grumpily, 'I was only thinking what a shame it is we can't stay at home in Kirrin Cottage after all!'

'Well, never mind,' said Julian. 'We'll only have to be away for two or three weeks, just so that Uncle Quentin and Professor Hayling can have time to finish their book in peace and quiet.'

'That's right,' agreed Dick. 'We're not being banished to Rose Cottage for so very long!'

'And just think of poor Uncle Quentin – he'd never get that important work of his done if he had us underfoot the whole time!' Anne reminded the others.

George suddenly smiled, and looked much better-tempered. 'Well, *you're* not the one who'd be most likely to disturb him!' she told Anne, truthfully. 'Nor Julian! But I suppose Dick and I do sometimes make rather a noise! And I know dear old Timmy can be *terribly* noisy when he feels like it. This is what comes of having a famous scientist for a father – you have to go about on tiptoe the whole time!'

'But it's just because Uncle Quentin and Aunt Fanny don't want to spoil our holidays by making us keep quiet that we're being sent to stay at Rose Cottage,' Julian pointed out. 'It's all turned out very well, really, seeing the Haylings' housekeeper, Jenny, owns the cottage, and she said she'd look after us if we went.'

'It doesn't look all that bad, either,' added Anne, glancing at the cottage beyond the garden gate.

The bicycle ride from Kirrin to Rose Cottage was only a couple of kilometres. Jenny's little house was a pretty white cottage, with green shutters at the windows, and the garden round it was full of trees, flowers and shrubs. They all grew in rather a wild, tangled way, but the garden still looked nice. No, it really wasn't a bad place at all!

'You're right, Anne!' George admitted. 'It *is* quite pretty.'

'And I bet we have some grand meals!' said Dick enthusiastically. 'You know what a wonderful cook Jenny is! She's bound to make us lovely cakes and buns and puddings – and we'll have Tinker to play with, too. Hello, there *is* Tinker!'

A boy about the same age as Dick and George came dashing out of the house like a bullet shooting from a gun, and ran to meet his friends.

'Good – here you are! Welcome to Rose Cottage!'

Professor Hayling's son was always known as Tinker, because he loved tinkering about with cars. The Professor himself was a famous scientist, like Uncle Quentin, and the two men were great friends. They often worked together, and this summer they had something very important to do – so to give them a bit of peace, Aunt Fanny had decided to send the children to stay with kind Jenny, the Haylings' housekeeper, who had looked after Tinker ever since his mother died.

Tinker opened the garden gate to let his friends in. 'I'm awfully glad my father's shut up our house at Big Hollow to go and stay at Kirrin Cottage,' he said. 'And he's let me come here to stay with *you*! This garden of Jenny's is a wonderful place for games. I've always loved playing Indians here!'

Jenny herself appeared on the white doorstep of the cottage. She was a plump little middle-aged woman, with a cheerful smile.

'Hello, children!' she said. 'Come along in! I've got a nice tea waiting for you – it will do you good after such a long bicycle ride!' She was joking of course!

George and her cousins laughed at that. But before they could say hello to Jenny, they heard a tremendous noise behind them.

'Woof! Woof!'

'Eeeak . . . chatter-chatter-chatter – *eeeak* . . . EEEAAK!'

George and Tinker burst out laughing.

'Listen to Timmy and Mischief saying hello!'

'Just like the old friends they are!'

Timmy was standing braced with all four paws planted firmly on the ground, while a little monkey gambolled affectionately round him. Mischief, Tinker's pet monkey, jumped up on the dog's back and then back down to the ground again, kissed Timmy's nose, and then repeated the whole performance, chattering away the whole time. Whenever the little monkey came within reach of Timmy's tongue, the dog gave him a friendly lick.

The two animals were really pleased to see each other, and went on playing until the children went indoors to sit down to a table covered with good things. There were egg sandwiches, Jenny's special home-made scones with cream and strawberry jam, and a big fruit cake. Soon Timmy came bouncing in to join the children, hoping for a sugar lump, and Mischief jumped up on Tinker's shoulder and begged for a biscuit.

As Jenny poured the tea, or milk for those who preferred it, she told the children, 'I don't know if Professor Hayling mentioned it, but I inherited this little cottage from my parents, and I thought I'd ask you to stay here because it's easier to look after than that big house of the Professor's at Big Hollow. But it will still take us all quite comfortably. Tinker's going to sleep in the big bedroom upstairs, with Julian and Dick, and there's another bedroom next to it for George and Anne to share.'

'We don't want to make a lot of extra work for you, Jenny, so we'll help in the house!' Anne promised. 'We'll make our own beds, and I'll dust the furniture.'

'Yes, and I'll lend a hand with the heavy jobs,' added good-natured Julian. 'I'm sure George and Dick will be delighted to volunteer for the washing up!'

George and Dick didn't *look* particularly delighted – but they both really had kind hearts, and they knew it was only right for them to help Jenny in the house when she had so many extra people to look after, so they agreed, in chorus, 'All right, we don't mind washing up!'

After tea – and washing up! – Tinker and the Five went to their rooms to unpack. They had brought small suitcases on the carriers of their bicycles, and when they had put their things away, they spent the rest of the day exploring the garden. It was wonderfully wild, and there was pretty countryside all round the cottage too.

'And Kirrin isn't very far away,' said George, 'so if we want to go and play on my island, we can always go back to Kirrin Cottage for my rowing boat! It's still tied up in its usual place.'

George was a very lucky girl: she had an island of her very own! It wasn't very far from the mainland, but you could describe it as a 'desert island' because nobody lived there – except the Five, now and then, when they went to camp on it. Uncle Quentin and Aunt Fanny had given George the island as a present. It still had the ruins of an old castle standing on it.

'You're right,' said Dick. 'You know, *I* think we'll really have more freedom here than if we'd stayed at Kirrin Cottage, George! I'm very fond of Uncle Quentin, but he does get a bit strict sometimes.'

'Yes, I must say Jenny's rather better-tempered than my father!' admitted George, smiling.

The last thing the friends did that evening was

to draw up a list of all the expeditions they were planning to make during the next few days, and then they went upstairs to bed.

They had soon settled in at Rose Cottage. Except when they were helping Jenny in the house, the children were free to do whatever they liked. It was lovely weather, and the fine spell looked like lasting. They bathed in the sea, went for cross-country hikes, played in the garden, and did all sorts of interesting things.

And then, one fine day – or rather, one *not* very fine day – the weather broke and it began to rain. The rain came down in a thin drizzle, cold and very wet, and it went on and on as if it was never going to stop. Fancy having weather like that in the summer holidays!

After the children had tried going out several times, only to come home drenched, and with Mischief's and Timmy's coats sticking to them, they gave it up and decided they'd just have to play indoor games to pass the time. But it did get boring, having to stay indoors, and Jenny had her work cut out keeping her guests happy. She was a kind soul, and didn't like it when the children were cross and snapped at each other, but where many grown-ups would have scolded or threatened to punish them if they didn't behave, Jenny knew a better way to stop them squabbling. She told them stories – she knew lots and lots of stories, all of them different and all very amusing. The children thoroughly enjoyed listening to her, because she had a real gift for story-telling. What tales she had to tell! Stories about the naughty things she used to do when she was a little girl, stories about her brothers and sisters, old tales about the local countryside – they were all fascinating!

But the rain went on and on.

'Oh dear,' sighed George, 'if only we could have an adventure! Or a nice little mystery to solve – at least then we'd have something to think about. If it goes on raining like this, our talents for adventure will rust up!'

'Leaving the Famous Five out of a job!' smiled Dick. 'Well, that'll be something new!'

Jenny, who was sitting quietly knitting, glanced out of the window.

'As to adventures and mysteries, I really couldn't say,' she remarked, 'but you *could* go for a nice outing! Look – the clouds are blowing away, and it's stopped raining at last. You don't want to stay shut indoors, pacing up and down. I know a good place where you could go for an expedition too!'

2

The Ruined Manor

George leaped to her feet.

'My goodness, Jenny, you're right! I never noticed the rain had stopped. I can't wait to get out of doors – let's take our bikes!'

'It would be better to go to the place I'm thinking of on foot,' Jenny told them. 'I thought you might like to have a look at the ruins of Mandeville Manor – it's a picturesque, round walk, and not a very long one. You could take your camera, Dick. I know you like taking photographs.'

'What way do we go for the round walk?' asked Julian.

'When you leave here, turn along the road to the left,' said Jenny. 'Walk on until you get to the ruins up on the hill – '

'Oh, are those the ruins of the old manor house?' cried Anne. 'We noticed them on our way here.'

'Yes, it was once the ancestral home of the

Mandeville family. They lived there for centuries, but then, at the time of the Civil War, Sir Rupert Mandeville was killed fighting for King Charles, and his wife had to flee the country with her son Hugh. That was when the house fell into disrepair.'

'Are there any of the family alive today?' asked Tinker.

'Oh yes! There's Mr Miles Mandeville, who's descended from Hugh, but not directly, so that's why he isn't "Sir Miles". He and his wife Sylvia are charming people. They have no children of their own, only a nephew called Benjamin, who will inherit the estate one day. I don't know him – he doesn't come here very often. The Mandevilles spend most of their time in London, but they travel a lot too. Mr Mandeville is an architect.'

'Do they live in the old ruins when they do come here?' asked Anne.

Dick roared with laughter, 'Don't be so silly, Anne! There isn't enough roof left on those ruins to keep a dormouse dry!'

Everyone else laughed too, including Anne, and Jenny shook her head.

'No – the family did go on living in the house for some time after the restoration of King Charles II, but there was never enough money to repair it properly – and just think what such a place would cost to keep up, too! When there was a big fire in the house about a hundred years ago, the family gave up living in it and let it fall into ruins. After Mr Miles Mandeville inherited the estate he had a nice, modern house of his own design built a little way off, in a picturesque part of the old park. It's called Wisteria Lodge.'

'Oh, I think we've seen that house too!' cried Anne. 'I'm sure we cycled past it.'

'The Mandeville estate itself is very large,' Jenny went on. 'Wisteria Lodge and its garden occupy only a very small part of it. The Mandevilles own all the countryside round the ruins too, and a lot of the land beside the main road, as well as Coney Wood and part of the land on which this very cottage is built!'

'What?' said Julian, surprised. 'You mean Rose Cottage itself is on the Mandeville estate?'

'Part of it! I believe that at the time of the Civil War, there was a hunting lodge where the cottage now stands – and even today, though Rose Cottage and the front garden are mine, the *back* garden really belongs to the Mandevilles! But they let me grow anything I like there. As I told you, Mr and Mrs Miles Mandeville are very nice people.'

'What else is there to see?' asked George. 'Besides the ruins, I mean.'

'Well, if you go up the hill there's a fine view of the sea. And there's an old prehistoric burial mound not far off – what they call a tumulus. You don't have to come back the way you went.

You can cut through Coney Wood, where there's a pretty little stream, with all sorts of wild flowers growing beside it.'

But just as the children were about to set off, something happened to delay them! Mischief decided that he'd like to borrow Timmy's collar. He took it off the dog's neck, and put it round his own! Good-tempered old Timmy didn't object. But as soon as Mischief was wearing the collar, the little monkey began to show off. He jumped around on the furniture, letting out his shrill chatter. Finally he leaped up on top of a tall cupboard and looked as if he was going to settle down there.

Tinker didn't think that was a good idea. He decided to get the little monkey down, so he put a chair on the table, and a stool on top of the chair, and then clambered up on them all, put out his hand – and tumbled down with a tremendous noise!

Luckily, he hadn't hurt himself, but Mischief was frightened. He jumped off his perch and caught hold of one arm of the light fitting hanging from the ceiling. It had several branches holding light bulbs. He swung there, looking ready to defy anyone. The children laughed and laughed, all except for poor Tinker, and Timmy barked.

Tinker, however, was very angry with Mischief, and went to fetch a broom to make the naughty monkey come down. He wasn't going to hit Mischief very hard with the broomstick, but the little monkey swerved to avoid it, lost his grip on the light fitting, slipped – and the dog collar, which was much too big for him, got caught on the branch he had been holding.

'Oh dear!' cried Anne in alarm. 'He'll strangle himself!'

Tinker was dashing about in a panic. George and her cousins ran to Jenny's boxroom. They knew she kept a pair of steps in there, so they fetched the steps, put them up under the light fitting, and Julian climbed up to unhook poor Mischief. Finally, George put Timmy's collar back on its rightful owner!

When all the excitement was over, the children looked out of the window and saw, to their dismay, that more dark clouds were coming up on the horizon.

'Oh well, never mind!' said George. 'Let's go out for a breath of fresh air anyway – if we just go as far as the ruins, then if it *does* rain again it won't be very far for us to run home!'

Jenny went to find their raincoats, and the children set off. Timmy was with them, of course, and so was Mischief, who had quickly recovered from his fright. He was clinging to Tinker's shoulder, snuggling close to his master.

The children walked at a brisk pace, and they were soon within sight of the ruined manor house.

It so happened that although the place wasn't really very far from Kirrin, they had never visited it before, and it did look interesting. They walked slowly all around the crumbling walls. Blackened stones showed where there had once been a fire – that would have been the one Jenny mentioned, about a hundred years ago. No doubt the house had fallen into decay even faster since then.

'I say, what a gloomy spot!' muttered Tinker. 'It's a pity Jenny told us the old cellars are all blocked up and we can't explore them – I love exploring cellars!'

The ruins were attractive but there wasn't a lot else to see. Weeds and climbing plants had taken over all that was left of the manor house, and George, her cousins, and Tinker had soon satisfied their curiosity.

'There isn't anything very exciting here after all!' said Dick, at last.

Julian glanced up at the sky. 'No – but I think we're in for some excitement in the way of a downpour if we stay much longer!' he said. 'We'd better hurry home.'

'Yes,' said George. 'We can do the round walk Jenny suggested some other time.'

'Oh dear, here comes the rain!' cried Anne. 'Let's run!'

And run they did! The children and Timmy made a dash for the road, but the rain beat them to it. It was really pouring down by the time they reached Rose Cottage and, having dried themselves – and Timmy – thoroughly, they spent the rest of the day playing board games indoors.

But next day it looked fine again, although it was more like April weather than summertime. The bright sunshine gave way to several sudden showers, and the children wished it would hurry and clear up properly!

That afternoon, as the sun suddenly shone out among the clouds again, Jenny told her young guests, 'Here's another sunny period, so you'd better make the most of it. Why not play in the orchard behind the house? You may be able to go for a real outing later on – showery weather like this often calms down towards the evening!'

'Orchard' was rather a grand name for the patch of grass in the back garden where a few apple trees grew, as well as a huge old oak, but it was a fine place for running about. The children organised a game of hide-and-seek, and Timmy and Mischief joined in with enthusiasm. The two animals were infected by the children's excitement. Timmy chased about, yapping and barking, and Mischief scurried all over the place, squealing and chattering like mad. They made no end of noise between them, but luckily Jenny hadn't got any neighbours living close to hear it!

Mischief decided the grass was too wet for his

liking, and suddenly he jumped up to the lowest branch of the big oak tree and began to climb. Once he was well up the tree, of course he didn't want to come down again.

'Mischief! Come down! Come on down!' shouted Tinker, but it was no good. He was afraid they were going to have a repeat performance of that comical scene the day before! 'Come down, or I'll have to come and get you, and then you'll be sorry!'

'Eeeak . . . eeeeak!' squealed the monkey in reply.

'Woof!' barked Timmy, in his deep voice, telling Mischief to come down too.

But nothing his master Tinker or his friend the dog said could persuade Mischief to leave his perch. Time was passing, and Jenny had already come out twice to call the children in to tea.

'Come *on*, Mischief!' Tinker repeated angrily.

'Why don't the rest of us go in?' suggested George. 'I'm sure he'll follow us then.'

'That's what *you* think! You don't know how pigheaded he can be!'

'Ever see a monkey with a pig's head before?' asked Dick, laughing like mad at his own joke. 'Well, if we're ever going to dislodge your pigheaded monkey from his tree, *I* think – '

But the others never found out what Dick thought, because before he could finish his sentence, there was a tremendous clap of thunder, and heavy rain began beating down on the orchard.

'Here comes another storm!' cried Julian. 'Back to the house, everyone – quick! There's lightning about, and it's dangerous to stay here under the trees.'

Startled by the noise, Mischief the monkey was already scampering down the tree as fast as he could go. Tinker held out his arms to catch him as he jumped, but the little monkey landed in the grass instead. In his fright, Mischief was thinking of nothing but reaching the nearest shelter, so instead of setting off for the cottage, he made straight for the far end of the orchard.

'Help me catch him!' Tinker called to his friends. 'You wicked monkey – I'm drenched already!'

They all began chasing Mischief through the driving rain. Timmy obviously thought this was a lovely new game, and came bounding up to join in. He was the first to reach Mischief – and then the children saw a surprising sight. Mischief jumped nimbly up on his friend's back, and Timmy ran on to the end of the orchard, just as if he were obeying his 'rider's' commands. They disappeared among some tall weeds.

'Oh, bother!' said George crossly.

She was just going to call Timmy, when Anne pointed. 'Look – I think their idea is to take refuge in the shed!'

She meant an old toolshed at the far end of the orchard. It wasn't often used now, but the children had found it and played houses in it a few times, and Jenny had let them take picnic meals there.

'Anne's right,' said Julian. 'Timmy and Mischief knew by instinct that the shed was closer than the house. Good idea – let's join them!'

By the time the children had reached the shed they were wet through. Rain was falling on the roof with a noise like hailstones now. Timmy and the monkey were obviously rather frightened – and very pleased to see George and Tinker. Mischief jumped into his master's arms, and Timmy pressed close to his mistress. A flash of lightning shot across the sky, followed by a tremendous clap of thunder, and then another and another.

'I say!' exclaimed Dick. 'What a storm!'

'That lightning was awfully close,' said Anne, sounding rather scared

'And the storm seems to be coming closer still!' said George, listening. The time between the flashes of lightning and the rolls of thunder was getting shorter and shorter. 'I wonder – '

But she didn't finish her sentence, because just then a tremendous flash lit up the shed, dazzling the children as they huddled together a little way inside the door. Almost at once, there was a deafening clap of thunder, and the ground seemed to shake beneath their feet. Timmy barked, and Mischief squealed in terror. George and the boys let out startled exclamations, and Anne screamed with fright.

'The cottage! It's been struck by lightning – oh, poor Jenny!' she gasped.

'Hush, Anne – calm down,' said Julian, soothingly. 'It's all right! Look – the lightning didn't touch the house, but it *did* strike the big oak in the middle of the orchard. See that?'

And sure enough, peering through the driving rain, the children saw that the magnificent old oak tree had gone – all that was left was a blackened column that had been its trunk, charred and smoking.

'My word!' said Tinker, turning pale. 'Just think – only a few minutes ago, Mischief was sitting on a branch of that tree!'

'And we were all standing underneath it, too,' added George.

3

Treasure!

The sound of the thunder was already dying away, and there were not so many flashes of lightning now. The storm was coming to an end.

The children heard Jenny's frightened voice, calling them. 'Tinker! Anne! George!'

'You stay here,' Julian told the others. 'I'll make a dash for the cottage, to let Jenny know we're okay, and then I'll be back with raincoats for all of us.'

He was back less than ten minutes later, running through the rain, and as well as the raincoats he had promised to bring he was carrying dry sweaters, and a big basket containing sandwiches, a huge chocolate cake, and thermos flask of hot cocoa.

'Jenny remembered the picnic cups and plates, too, so we can camp out here very comfortably until the storm's really over!' said Julian.

So they had an unexpected and very cheerful picnic. Timmy and Mischief were feeling hungry too, so the delicious picnic tea Jenny had packed in the basket was soon gone. Not a crumb was left.

'Gosh – I feel better now!' said Dick. 'It was pretty exciting, though, wasn't it? I say, I think the rain's stopped. Let's go and take a closer look at the damage that thunderbolt did!'

When they emerged from the shed, the children saw that the sun had come out again, and the wind was chasing the clouds away. They were certainly having changeable weather!

'My word, there's not much of that huge oak left now,' said George, rather sadly. 'What a shame – it was such a fine tree!'

'Yes, and while she was packing up our picnic just now, Jenny told me it's one of the few trees on the Mandeville estate supposed to date back to the time when Sir Rupert and Lady Mandeville lived at the Manor before the Civil War,' said Julian.

The children looked at the place where the tree used to stand with even more interest than before. They saw that when the thunderbolt struck, it had dug a sort of circular crater all round the charred stump of the tree.

'Look how deep it is,' said Tinker. 'It would take ages for anyone to dig a hole like that themselves – and they'd have got blisters on their hands, too.'

Mischief, feeling playful again, jumped down into the hole. He seemed to have spotted something interesting, because he started digging away in the earth with his tiny hands. Timmy jumped in too, to help him, and began scraping soil aside with his paws.

'Do look at them – they're playing Hunt the Thimble, or something!' said Tinker, laughing.

But George had a thoughtful frown on her face. She bent down to get a better look inside the hole. She had heard the dog's claws scrape against something hard, buried in the ground – and then she heard the same sound again. What could it be? George felt intrigued.

'Seek, Timmy! Good dog – go on, seek!' she told her dog.

Hearing the encouraging note in her voice, Timmy dug harder than ever. Suddenly, all the children let out exclamations. The dog's busy paws had just uncovered something – something dull-coloured and rusty, but easy to recognise. It was the lid of a metal casket.

'Hello!' said Dick. 'I wonder what that is?'

'Perhaps it's buried treasure!' said Anne, just for a joke.

'An old dustbin lid, more likely!' said Tinker.

Dick and George were already down in the hole with Timmy, trying to tug the metal box out of the earth. But it was well embedded, and they couldn't get a good grip on it anywhere.

'Wait a sec!' said Julian. 'I'll go and fetch some tools!'

He ran back to the toolshed, and came back with
a spade and a pickaxe. He and Dick soon managed
to dig the box up and hoist it out of the hole. George
lifted the lid – that was easy enough, because rust
had eaten away the lock and the hinges.

And then they all exclaimed again, in sheer
amazement!

'I don't believe it! It really *is* buried treasure!'

'Gold! Gold and jewels!'

'Golly – there must be a fortune in there!'

'Just pinch me, will you, Dick? So I know I'm
not dreaming!' George asked her cousin.

Dick was quite ready to oblige – and she *wasn't*
dreaming. She was gazing at a wonderful treasure,
the kind of thing you'd expect to find only in a
storybook.

The Five had already found valuable lost or
stolen property on a number of occasions – but
only after they had worked hard searching and
making inquiries. This was the first time they had
ever stumbled across such riches quite by chance,
without having to go to any trouble at all! They were
dazzled!

'I tell you what – it somehow doesn't seem *right*!'
said George to the others. 'Fancy finding a treasure
like this, just by accident!'

'A bolt from the blue!' said Dick, laughing.

Julian quickly pulled himself together.

'Come on, let's take this box into Rose Cottage

and show it to Jenny,' he said. 'I wonder who can have buried it in the orchard? Perhaps she'll know.'

Jenny looked relieved when the children came in. 'So there you are at last!' she said. 'I was just beginning to worry about you. Are you terribly wet?'

'Never mind about that!' Tinker interrupted, impatient to show off their find. 'See what we've got here!'

Julian and Dick put the box on the kitchen table and opened it – and Jenny's mouth dropped open as she stared at the contents. It was at least half a minute before she could utter a word.

'My goodness, children!' she said at last. 'It can't be possible – why, I can hardly believe my eyes! So it really *did* exist! Oh, goodness gracious me! Won't Mr Mandeville be pleased! And what a shame poor Hugh Mandeville couldn't benefit from it, all those years ago.'

It was the children's turn to be baffled. 'What are you talking about, Jenny?' asked George.

'Why, the Mandeville treasure, of course! The lost treasure! Didn't I tell you that part of the story? It all happened so long ago, you see.'

'Tell us *now*, Jenny – quick, tell us!' cried Tinker.

'Well, do you remember how I was telling you, the other day, about Lady Mandeville and her son Hugh, who was only a little boy at the time of the Civil War? My own family has lived round here

for hundreds of years too, you see, and one of
my distant ancestors, called Andrew Foster, was a
servant of Lady Mandeville's in those days. That's
how I come to know the Mandevilles' family history
so well. Lady Mandeville was quite a young woman
when she was widowed, and beautiful too. It was
very sad for her when Sir Rupert was killed fighting
for the King – and when the Roundheads became
very powerful in this part of the country, she didn't
feel safe any more.'

'Not even in her own home?' asked Dick.

'No, because, you see, her husband had always
supported King Charles, and she knew that all the
people hereabouts who supported Cromwell would
bear her a grudge too.'

Anne couldn't help shivering. 'Oh, poor Lady
Mandeville!' she said.

'And more and more people were going over to
Cromwell all the time, now that he was winning the
war,' Jenny went on. 'Soon the whole of this part of
the country was in turmoil. Andrew Foster was still
able to go between the manor house and the village,
and he told Lady Mandeville she was in danger. He
was devoted to the Mandeville family himself, and
he advised her to escape at once, taking her little
boy with her. Lady Mandeville knew he was right.
She decided to go to France, like a great many other
aristocratic people about that time, including the
King's son himself. At least she and Hugh would

be safe in France, though she hoped they wouldn't have to stay there long.'

'Where does this treasure come into the story, though, Jenny?' Tinker prompted her.

'Well, before she left the Mandevilles' ancestral home, Lady Mandeville hid her gold and jewels, with Andrew Foster's help,' Jenny said. 'She dared not take them with her, for fear they'd be stolen, and if she left them behind it was more than likely the house itself might be ransacked. So she took only what she knew she would need, put the rest in a casket, and Andrew found a good place to hide it. Lady Mandeville and young Hugh watched him bury the treasure, and then they all went away to France. Faithful old Andrew wasn't going to be left behind! But poor Lady Mandeville died abroad, and so did Andrew Foster – Hugh was brought up by friends in France, and many years later he came back to England on his own. He found the manor house empty and derelict, and he couldn't tell where the treasure was buried. Hard as he searched, he never did find it!'

'Why not?' asked George. 'You mean he just couldn't remember where to look?'

'No – Hugh had been very small when Andrew Foster buried the treasure, and all he could remember was watching the old man dig a hole somewhere in the grounds while he and his mother looked on.'

'But didn't Lady Mandeville or old Andrew

tell him where to look, before they died?' asked Dick.

'Lady Mandeville died very suddenly, you see – it was said she left her son some family papers, and I expect they gave a clue to the whereabouts of the treasure but they were lost. People in France wouldn't have thought much of papers written in English – and this was a time when most people couldn't read or write at all, remember! Oh, dear me, children – just to think that the Mandeville treasure has been lying under the big oak tree all this time! And but for you, and the thunderstorm, it would still be there!'

'But how can we be sure it really *is* the Mandeville fortune?' asked George.

Jenny looked at the open casket and picked something up. 'There's no doubt about that!' she said. 'Look – here's a miniature painted on ivory, showing a little boy, with his name written underneath. Hugh Mandeville! To tell you the truth, my dears, I didn't entirely believe in the existence of the treasure myself. People have talked about it for so long, you see, and yet nobody has ever found it. And now you children just stumble across it! George, we ought to let your father know, and then I'm sure he'll see to it that Mr Miles Mandeville gets his ancestors' fortune back. Why, I believe Mr and Mrs Mandeville are returning home today – how lucky!'

George said nothing. She didn't want to leave it

to her father! She wanted to get in touch with the owners of Wisteria Lodge herself, and see their faces when she gave them the precious treasure Timmy had dug up on their land.

'Let's make a list of all the things in the box,' suggested Tinker. 'You know – what they call an inventory! That would be fun.'

It *was* fun, and very exciting, too. The children counted over six hundred gold coins with the head of King Charles I on them, and there was a whole set of emerald jewellery, a diamond and sapphire bracelet, a huge, unset ruby, a tiara, a diamond pendant, and a great many rings and earrings set with precious stones. Then there was an enormous pear-shaped pearl, three engraved gold bracelets, three gold chains, two gold watches and chains, four medallions, several miniatures painted on ivory – among them that picture of little Hugh, and another of his mother – and a signet ring with the arms of the Mandeville family on the seal. That certainly proved whose the treasure was.

'Are you sure Mr Mandeville and his wife are at Wisteria Lodge now?' Dick asked the housekeeper.

'Well, that's what they were saying in the grocer's earlier today – the Mandevilles were expected to arrive about ten o'clock this morning.'

George glanced out of the window. 'The storm's quite finished now – why don't we go and tell them the news?' she suggested.

'Yes, that's a good idea!' Julian agreed. 'We must leave the casket here in Jenny's care, of course. It wouldn't be safe to go carrying all those precious things round on our bicycles! But if the Mandevilles don't want to come straight over and fetch the treasure themselves, I'm sure Uncle Quentin or Professor Hayling will take it over to them by car if we ask them to.'

'Yes, and don't you remember? Aunt Fanny is coming to see us tomorrow!' Anne said. 'Maybe she'd like to take it back to them. Oh yes, George, do let's cycle over to Wisteria Lodge and tell the Mandevilles what we've found!'

With such good news to tell, the children cycled fast and energetically. Vapour was steaming up from the wet ground in the hot sunshine, and the clouds were all blowing away at last. George and Dick led the little procession, with Timmy running along beside them. Julian, Tinker and Anne followed, more sedately, but they were all keen to get to Wisteria Lodge and see Miles and Sylvia Mandeville. What a lovely surprise for the architect and his wife! The children could just imagine their amazement and delight.

But sad to say, things didn't turn out exactly as they expected . . .

— 4 —

The Disagreeable Caretaker

The children cycled past the ruined manor house, and soon saw the white paint of Wisteria Lodge ahead of them. It was a square, pleasant house, with pretty purple wisteria and other climbing plants growing over it. There were neat flower beds and well mown lawns in the gardens. The children looked through the railings and saw a man walking along the garden path. When Julian pulled a chain hanging by the garden gateway, a bell rang in the distance.

The man in the garden stopped, turned round, and then came towards the gate. They heard the gravel of the path crunching under his feet.

'Good – here comes somebody!' said Dick. Like George, he was so excited he could hardly keep still.

When the man reached the gate, they could see that he was middle-aged, with thin, greying hair.

His face was rather forbidding, and he had a thin-lipped mouth. He didn't smile at the children. George noticed that he was wearing corduroy trousers and a blue overall.

The man looked at the children. He didn't seem to be in any hurry to open the gate.

'What do you want?' he asked.

'We'd like to see Mr Mandeville!' said George eagerly. 'Is he at home?'

The man did not reply at once. He was looking hard at the children, and finally he seemed to make his mind up. 'My employer doesn't talk to strange kids!' he said. 'He's got better things to do!'

George opened her mouth to protest, but he went on, 'I'm the caretaker here, and it's my job to keep unwanted visitors out!' He spoke in a most unpleasant tone of voice.

George went crimson with rage! Patience was not her strong point anyway, and the way the caretaker was behaving was really infuriating. 'I'd have thought it was up to Mr Mandeville to say if he wants to see us or not,' she said, doing her best not to lose her temper. 'So would you go and tell him we'd like to talk to him? We have something extremely important to say to him!'

The caretaker began to laugh. 'Well, well, well!' he said sarcastically. 'Just hark at the lad! Sharp-tongued, aren't you? And impertinent too! Well, well – and just who do you think you are, my boy?'

George felt her temper rise to boiling point. Of course, it wasn't at all unusual for people to think she really *was* a boy, and she did look like one. Most of the time she didn't mind a bit – in fact, she rather liked it. But she didn't care for being treated as a cheeky brat by this horrible man! She was about to answer when Julian, realising that she was about to explode, hastily stepped in.

'You're making a mistake,' he told the caretaker coldly. 'My cousin here, Miss Georgina Kirrin, really has got some very important news for Mr Mandeville, so would you kindly let him know we're here?'

The caretaker looked suspiciously at the children again, and they could tell he wasn't quite sure what to do now. However, it didn't look as if he was going to oblige Julian, so Dick thought he'd put a word in too. 'That's right!' he said. 'And it's very, very *good* news we've got for Mr Mandeville, too!'

Anne spoke up as well. 'Oh yes!' she said, with her nicest smile. 'Please do believe my brothers! It really is *very* good news – about the lost treasure! We've found – '

George quickly interrupted, glaring at her cousin. 'Be quiet, Anne, you little chatterbox!' she snapped.

Realising how thoughtlessly she had been chattering away, the little girl blushed and bit her lip.

But George's warning came too late. The caretaker had caught what Anne said, and he was certainly interested now! His manners improved as if by magic, and his voice became gentler.

'Treasure? What treasure?' he asked. 'You don't mean the Mandeville treasure said to have been buried by old Andrew Foster during the Civil War, do you?'

None of the children felt like telling him any more. Anne hung her head. She would have given a lot to take back the words she'd so stupidly let slip! Seeing that they were all silent, the man went on, 'I think you *do* mean Lady Mandeville's treasure! Am I right?'

George looked him up and down. 'We don't want to talk to you – only to Mr Mandeville!' she said firmly. 'Now, are you or aren't you going to let us see him? Make up your mind!'

A gleam came into the caretaker's eyes. 'It's like this, children,' he said in a much gentler tone than before. 'Mr and Mrs Mandeville aren't at home at the moment – they won't be back until tonight, or maybe tomorrow, or they might even be staying for a day or so longer. I think it would be best if you told me your story, since they're not here. Well – what's it all about?'

He wasn't so cross now, but Julian didn't like his manner any better than before. Timmy was sniffing the man's shoes through the railings, and growling quietly. *He* didn't take to the caretaker any more than George did.

'Sorry, but that's our business – and Mr Mandeville's,' said Julian firmly. 'Well, we'll just have to come back tomorrow, and the day after too if necessary.'

'Oh, it really isn't worth your while to put yourselves to all that trouble,' protested the caretaker. 'You might have a wasted journey, too. Why not give me your address? Then I can let you know as soon as Mr and Mrs Mandeville get back!'

It was Tinker who put his foot in it this time! He was slow to realise that his friends didn't want to tell the caretaker any more than he already knew, and without meaning any harm, he let out the information the man was after.

'My name's Tinker Hayling,' he said, 'and I'm staying at Rose Cottage with my friends here – perhaps you know where it is?'

'Why yes, I certainly do! I often pass the cottage on my way down to the village, so just leave it to me! I'll drop a note into your letter-box as soon as Mr Mandeville comes home.'

The caretaker was smiling now. George thought she rather preferred his rudeness to that sugary smile!

On the way back from Wisteria Lodge, she told her cousins and Tinker, 'That man was really horrible! I didn't like him a little bit.'

'We shouldn't judge by appearances, you know,' said Julian, who had a strong sense of fair play. 'He may be kind at heart, even if he has a surly sort of way with him.'

But George wasn't convinced. 'Well, Timmy agrees with me,' she said. 'I could tell that *he* couldn't stand the man either. And believe me, Ju, old Timmy isn't often wrong about that sort of thing. You can rely on his instinct!'

Dick agreed with his cousin. 'He was working in the garden – how do we know he's really a caretaker at the house at all, and not just a gardener who was trying to make out he was Mr Mandeville's right-hand man so as to gain our confidence? I didn't take to him at all!'

'Nor did I! He didn't begin to sound polite until the moment Anne mentioned the treasure,' said Tinker. 'Honestly, Anne, how *could* you be so silly?'

'No sillier than you, old chap!' Julian pointed out gently. 'Why on earth did you have to go and give that man our address?'

Tinker looked at Julian, puzzled. 'What's that got to do with it?'

Dick explained. 'Tinker, we didn't want the man to know where he could find us – and the treasure!'

'Oh dear – yes, I see now,' said Tinker ruefully.

'Well, there's no point in arguing!' interrupted George. 'It's no use crying over spilt milk, either! The important thing now is to keep a close watch on that precious casket until my mother arrives tomorrow and we can get her help.'

'Yes, George is right,' said Anne. 'I expect Aunt Fanny will tell Uncle Quentin, and he'll come to fetch the treasure, and then it will be safe.'

When they got back to Rose Cottage, the children told Jenny about the disappointing result of their expedition.

'Oh, I know the man you mean,' the housekeeper told them. 'Yes, he's caretaker and gardener at Wisteria Lodge all right – his name is Johnson, and he's fairly new to these parts – nobody seems to like him much round here! He's rather sly, and mean too. In fact, I don't know why the Mandevilles employ him, but as they aren't here so very often, perhaps they don't know what he's like – and they're very kind-hearted, too. Too kind-hearted for their own good, if you ask me.'

Next morning the children had another disappointment. Aunt Fanny telephoned to say she had a slight cold, and so she didn't think it would be a good idea for her to come and see the children that day after all. 'I'd better stay indoors, George,' she told her daughter, 'and then I'll soon be well again.'

'Can *we* come and see *you*?' asked George.

'That wouldn't be very sensible either – since you're out of reach of my germs at Rose Cottage, I don't want to pass them to you! I'll see you in a few days' time, dear!' And Aunt Fanny hung up, sneezing, before George could say any more.

'You didn't mention the treasure,' said Julian, who had been standing beside her.

'No, I didn't get time! But I've been thinking why *don't* we take it to the Mandevilles ourselves, after all? We can walk instead of bicycling to Wisteria Lodge, and we'll take jolly good care not to hand it over until we actually see Mr or Mrs Mandeville in person.'

Julian didn't look as if he thought this was a very good idea – but before he or the others could say anything about it, Mischief had darted off to the garden gate. He had seen a piece of white paper lying in the letter-box fastened to the gate itself, and he was soon back, triumphantly clutching an envelope in his little paw. He held it out to Tinker. The note was addressed to Miss Kirrin and Mr Hayling. The envelope turned out to contain a card with Mr Mandeville's name at the top, and the message on the card was very brief.

'Mr Mandeville regrets that he is too busy to come to see you himself or to ask you to visit him. However, his nephew, Benjamin Latchford, will call on you today before noon, to thank you on Mr Mandeville's behalf. Would you be good enough to give Mr Latchford what you have found?'

The note was signed 'Miles Mandeville'.

'Well!' said George, disgusted. 'How *rude*! Short

and not very sweet – not only can Mr Mandeville not be bothered to see us himself, he's hardly even saying thank you!'

Dick shook his head. 'If you ask me, he doesn't believe in the treasure!' he said. 'Goodness knows what that caretaker man, Johnson, has told him about us! He probably said we're just kids playing a practical joke, or something like that! So Mr Mandeville doesn't trust us, or believe we've got anything worth his while.'

'I think Dick is right,' Julian agreed. 'Mr Mandeville wouldn't want to run the risk of looking silly by dashing off after a treasure that doesn't really exist!'

'But it jolly well *does* exist!' said Anne, glancing at a shabby little suitcase on the floor. Jenny had thought it might be a good idea to hide the casket inside this suitcase for camouflage.

George sighed. 'Oh well, we'll just have to wait here for Mr Mandeville's nephew. Still, fancy just sending someone else to collect such a treasure! I really do think he's being offhand about it, don't you?'

So the Five, Tinker and Mischief spent the morning in the garden, keeping an eye on the gate. They were eagerly waiting for Benjamin Latchford to appear. They rather looked forward to the moment when they'd show him all the precious things, and see his face when he realised that the treasure *was* real, whatever his uncle thought – and fabulously valuable!

It was still well before noon when they heard the noise of a motor-bike coming along the road. That must be Benjamin, they all felt sure!

— 5 —

Benjamin – or is it?

Sure enough, the motorbike stopped outside Rose Cottage, and a tall, thin, dark-haired young man of about eighteen got off it. He rang the bell.

The children all went to open the gate. 'You the kids, are you?' asked the newcomer. 'I'm Benjamin Latchford.'

George frowned. She didn't much like the young man's high-and-mighty tone, nor the way he called them 'kids' – it was as if he didn't think they were worth his attention! But Tinker went up to the motorcyclist.

'Yes,' he said. 'We're the people who discovered your family's ancestral treasure!'

'Well, that's wonderful! My uncle will be delighted. Let's have a look at the loot, then!'

It was Julian's turn to frown. He didn't take to this Benjamin at all. He thought his manner was very offhand and unattractive. All the same, he politely introduced the others – not forgetting Timmy, who had been the first to sniff out that casket full of gold and jewels.

Benjamin Latchford listened with obvious impatience, and he seemed very tense, although the children couldn't think why. But a gleam came into his eyes when Julian mentioned the gold and jewels. He still didn't smile, though, and Anne noticed that he was involuntarily clenching and unclenching his fists as he said curtly, 'Okay, now show me the goods, will you? I haven't got much time, and my uncle's waiting.'

The children led Benjamin to the cottage door, and Jenny welcomed him in her usual friendly way. However, Timmy was growling softly and sniffing at the visitor's ankles.

'Oho!' George thought with amusement, 'it looks as if Timmy doesn't like Benjamin any more than we do!'

Jenny produced the suitcase and put it on the living room table, Julian opened it, Dick lifted out the rusty old casket, and George unpacked all the wonderful things inside it. They certainly *did* impress Benjamin, just as the children had expected. He let out a low whistle of amazement.

'Crikey!' he exclaimed. 'How about that for a real little gold-mine!'

Julian was surprised by Benjamin's behaviour. He was clearly not the perfect gentleman Jenny said his uncle was. Benjamin got over his surprise, briskly swept the gold coins and jewellery into a heap and put them into the casket again, and returned the casket itself to Jenny's old suitcase.

'Well, I'll be off now, and take this straight to my uncle,' he said. And he was about to pick up the suitcase and walk out with it.

Jenny hesitated. She had an uneasy feeling that something wasn't quite right, and she did wish Aunt Fanny was there. Julian, Dick and Anne glanced at each other, not sure what to do. Anne wondered why they were so quiet all of a sudden.

Then George stepped forward, placing herself between Benjamin and the door. 'Wait a minute!' she said. 'Mr Mandeville certainly told us his nephew Benjamin Latchford would be calling, and he did ask us to hand over the treasure to Benjamin. But I hope you won't mind if we ask you to prove your identity! After all, we don't know you, do we?'

'My cousin's quite right,' said Julian. 'Have you got any documents on you to prove who you are – a driving licence or anything like that?'

The boy went pale, and shot a furious glance at the two cousins. 'How dare you speak to me like that? I *am* Miles Mandeville's nephew!' he shouted.

'Okay, then prove it!' said Dick, walking over to stand with his own back to the door. 'And if you don't happen to have any proof with you, I expect you can go and find some papers to back up your claim, and *then* we'll hand over the treasure!'

'Oh, very well! I'll go straightaway!'

'But put that suitcase down first,' Tinker told him.

However, instead of obeying, the young man made for the door. Julian, Dick, and George barred his way. With a shout of fury, he swung round, pushing Jenny aside, and fending off Anne and Tinker as they tried to grab hold of him. He was making for the window!

But he had reckoned without Timmy. The good dog, who had been sniffing round the stranger, growling, all this time, sprang at him, caught him by his leather jacket, braced himself on all four paws, and clung on with all his might.

The fake Benjamin – for by now it was clear to all of them that this young man was an impostor – turned, dropped the suitcase, and tried to pull the dog off him. It was no good! Timmy let go of the jacket for a moment, but only to take a firm hold of the seat of his jeans. With a growl of triumph, he tore away a big piece of denim – and maybe a little bit of skin too, because the young man let out a howl!

As 'Benjamin' made for the door, abandoning the suitcase, George held it open for him with a mock-polite gesture. He rushed out, clutching his behind with both hands. The children were in fits of laughter! Then Mischief decided that *he* would take a hand too. Jumping up on the fugitive's shoulder, the little monkey climbed on to his head and began pulling his hair very hard. The young man howled louder than ever, and ran for it, disappearing from the children's sight. But a moment later, they and Jenny heard the sound of his motorbike starting up, and Mischief soon reappeared, looking very pleased with himself. He started chattering away to Timmy in shrill tones, no doubt telling his friend all about his brave deeds!

When the children's laughter had died down a bit, Dick said, 'Well, that was a close shave! The Mandeville treasure would have fallen into quite the wrong hands but for you, George.'

'But for Timmy, you mean,' said George, patting her dog.

Julian had stopped laughing now, and was frowning instead as he thought it all over. 'How did that young man who was pretending to be Benjamin Latchford know that Mr Mandeville's nephew was going to call here this morning?' he said. 'He was running quite a risk, wasn't he, counting on getting here first!'

George shook her head. 'If you ask me, the real Benjamin won't turn up at all,' she said. 'The whole message telling us to expect him was probably faked!'

'What do you mean?' asked Anne and Tinker.

'I mean it almost certainly wasn't Mr Mandeville who sent us that curt, rude note! Jenny says he's such a gentleman! We ought to have suspected something from the start.'

'Then who did write it?' asked Tinker.

'I can only think of one likely person,' said George, 'and that's Johnson, the caretaker at Wisteria Lodge. After all, *he's* the only one who knows we've found Lady Mandeville's treasure.'

'But he didn't come for it himself,' Tinker protested.

'No – he knew we wouldn't hand it over to him, so he sent an accomplice instead! I don't think we need expect to see the real Benjamin today.'

They did wait until twelve noon, however. But sure enough, nobody else turned up. All the evidence showed that George had guessed right.

'Oh dear, that Johnson is a real bad lot!' sighed Jenny. 'I do wish he didn't know you've got the treasure, children.'

'Well, we must do something!' said George briskly. 'Perhaps Johnson was lying to us, and Mr Mandeville is at home after all. If so, we'll try to see him again – that will be one in the eye for Johnson!'

So directly after lunch, the children got on their bicycles and went off to Wisteria Lodge, followed by Timmy, as usual. When they reached the garden gate they dismounted. Much to their disappointment, all the windows of the house were closed, and the place looked shut up. Julian rang the bell by the gate, but nobody appeared, not even Johnson.

Feeling rather flat, the five friends looked at each other. They decided to wait a little longer, in case somebody came home, but it didn't look as if Mr Mandeville was back yet after all. It was really very frustrating! Then a girl came along the road with a basket of eggs.

'Looking for somebody?' she asked the children. 'If it's the Mandevilles you want to see, you'll have to wait another twenty-four hours. They're still in London, but they expect to be back tomorrow. Our farm is just along the road, and they've written to my father to order milk every morning from then on.'

That sounded like better news! George and the others thanked the girl, and when she had disappeared round the next corner, Dick cried, 'So you *were* right, George! If Mr Mandeville isn't here, he couldn't have written us that note, and it must have been Johnson who did!'

The children stood by the garden gate for a few minutes longer, working things out. 'I wonder who the fake Benjamin really is?' Tinker wondered. 'I just hope that once Mr Mandeville hears about all this, he'll be asking his caretaker a few questions. And getting answers to them, too!'

'What are we going to do until he gets back?' said Anne, worried.

'Nothing,' said George. 'We must just wait! We'll come back here tomorrow, and *then* we should be able to talk to the owner of Wisteria Lodge.'

'But meanwhile we ought to make sure the treasure's safe. Maybe we ought to hand it over to the police,' suggested Julian, who was the most thoughtful and sensible of all the children.

'Oh no, please, Ju!' begged George. She really *did* want to give it to the Mandevilles in person! 'I mean, it would be silly, just for such a short time – and think how pleased Mr Mandeville will be to have his inheritance back without any formal fuss and bother!'

'But that means we have to keep it for another twenty-four hours – and we'll be responsible if anything happens to it,' Julian pointed out, sounding very worried.

'Twenty-four hours isn't long!' said Dick, who always tended to back George up. 'Who do you think would go off with it?'

'Have you forgotten that Johnson and that young man pretending to be Benjamin have already tried going off with it?' asked Julian.

'No, of course not, but they'll never have the nerve to try again! Why don't we hide the treasure somewhere safe until it's time to hand it back to the rightful owner?'

'Good idea!' agreed Tinker, getting on his bicycle. 'Let's go home, quick, and find it a safe hiding place!'

— 6 —

A Safe Hiding Place

The children cycled back fast, in a great hurry to put the precious treasure somewhere safe. They only hoped nothing had happened to it while they were out!

However, when they reached Rose Cottage everything was all right. But Jenny told them she was very worried. 'I just don't feel easy in my mind, children, with all those golden coins and precious stones about! Such a fortune to have in the house!'

'It'll be off our hands tomorrow, Jenny!' said Tinker. 'And meanwhile, we're going to hide it so well that the cleverest of thieves couldn't find it!'

First of all, George, Julian, Dick, Anne and Tinker took the case containing the precious casket up to the attic. Dick had suggested slipping it under one of the beams there, but they found the case would stick out quite a long way, so that anyone could see it, and they dropped that idea.

Then Anne asked why they didn't put it inside a trunk – but Tinker pointed out that would be one of the very first places where a burglar would look for it. Julian and George suggested that they should try the cellar, so they all went downstairs again.

'I know – let's hide the treasure in the boiler!' said Julian. 'It's not on at the moment, because it's summertime, and it would make a grand safe!'

But although the suitcase wasn't very big, it was still too large to go through the opening of the boiler, and they soon gave up the attempt to get it in. George suggested simply stuffing it under the old sacks piled against the end wall of the cellar, and putting an old bedstead in front of it. Everyone agreed to this idea, and George began directing operations.

'Julian and Dick, you take one end of the bedstead each,' she said. 'Pick it up carefully and put it down over here, and whatever you do, mind you don't drag it over the floor.'

Tinker was looking puzzled. 'Why all these precautions?' he asked.

'Because if we go dragging the bedstead over the dusty floor it'll leave marks,' George explained. 'Then anyone will be able to see straight away that it's been moved, and it'll be an obvious place to look for something hidden!'

'You think of everything, George!' said Anne admiringly.

Tinker helped the other boys move the bedstead.

Still taking care not to leave any tracks, George picked up the dusty sacks and hid the suitcase behind them.

'There!' she said, straightening up. 'Now the treasure's safely hidden, and all we have to do is put the bedstead in position in front of it!'

No sooner said than done! Then, with their minds at rest, the children went off to the kitchen, where Jenny had made them a delicious tea, with a big plate of chocolate biscuits as a special treat. That put them in a good mood again, and the rest of the day passed pleasantly if uneventfully.

At breakfast next morning, the children discussed the best way of getting in touch with the Mandevilles at Wisteria Lodge.

'If I were you I'd telephone instead of just turning up on the doorstep,' said Jenny. 'If you arrive too early, maybe nobody will answer the door – or you might meet that Johnson again, and find he won't let you in!'

'Yes, why don't we telephone?' cried Tinker. 'That's a good idea – we ought to have thought of it before!'

'What's the Mandevilles' number?' asked George.

'I don't know, but you're sure to find it in the telephone book,' said Jenny. 'I should call at about ten o'clock, I think.'

The children took Jenny's advice, and at ten

o'clock, George picked up the telephone and dialled the number of Wisteria Lodge.

A man's deep, pleasant voice replied.

'This is Georgina Kirrin speaking,' said George, very distinctly. 'I'd like to talk to Mr Miles Mandeville, please. It's personal!'

'Miles Mandeville here,' said the voice, sounding a little amused. 'Go ahead – I'm listening!'

So in a few sentences, George told the tale of their amazing adventure, and the fabulous treasure they had discovered.

For a moment or so, Mr Mandeville said nothing at all. Then he began, 'If this is some kind of joke – '

'No honestly it isn't!' George protested. 'It's nothing but the truth! If you'll let us come and see you, we'll explain all about it, and then you can come back to Rose Cottage with us and we'll hand over your property.'

There was another moment's silence at the other end of the line, and then Mr Mandeville said, 'Very well! I'll expect you at Wistaria Lodge at about three this afternoon – but I must say, your story sounds very strange to me!'

With a sigh of relief, George put the receiver down again. 'Phew! Done it!' she told the others. 'Mr Mandeville will see us this afternoon!'

The children were very excited. They stayed in the garden of Rose Cottage all morning, looking forward to their meeting with the Mandevilles that afternoon. Anne, who loved pretty things, kept imagining Sylvia Mandeville's delight when she saw the jewels.

'She'll be so pleased and happy! I can just see her putting on that diamond tiara, like a queen wearing a crown – '

'And then going out to do her shopping in it, I suppose!' finished Tinker, laughing.

The children were still in the garden when the bell rang at about eleven. A tall, distinguished-looking man stood at the garden gate.

'I'd like to see Miss Georgina Kirrin, please,' he said politely. 'I believe she's staying here, isn't she?'

George stepped forward. 'I'm Georgina Kirrin – oh, I bet you're Mr Mandeville!'

The visitor smiled. 'Yes, that's right! Forgive me for coming over on impulse like this, but when I thought about it, I hadn't got the patience to wait until this afternoon to meet you and your friends!'

George smiled, with a mischievous gleam in her eye. She guessed that Mr Mandeville, doubting the truth of her story and afraid that someone was trying to play a trick on him, had come to make sure for himself that the children really *did* live at Rose Cottage, as she had said, and weren't just anonymous practical jokers. But she was too well brought up to say exactly what she was thinking out loud!

First of all she introduced her cousins and Tinker, not forgetting Mischief and Timmy too.

'It's thanks to my dog Timmy we found your family treasure at all, Mr Mandeville,' she said. 'But for him, we'd never have guessed there was anything there!'

The children could tell that Mr Mandeville still wasn't quite sure whether or not to believe them, so they invited him to follow them into the cottage, where Professor Hayling's housekeeper confirmed their amazing story.

'Yes, sir, Miss Georgina has told you the exact truth,' said dear old Jenny. 'When the children brought in that rusty old casket after the storm, I could hardly believe my eyes. All those gold coins! And the jewels – precious stones all sparkling with different colours! It was like something in a fairy tale!'

Mr Mandeville seemed quite staggered by what Jenny told him. 'This is astonishing!' he said. 'To think of my ancestral inheritance being found quite by accident, after such a long time! Forgive me if I seem a little upset, but I can scarcely get over it!'

Julian nodded sympathetically. 'We understand, sir! It certainly must make you feel odd!'

'But you just wait till you see the treasure for yourself!' added Dick, cheerfully.

'We hid it down in the cellar, for fear of jewel thieves,' explained Tinker.

'Jewel thieves?' said Mr Mandeville, smiling. 'I don't imagine there are many jewel thieves about in this quiet part of the country! And I suppose you didn't tell anyone else you were looking after such a fabulous treasure!'

Anne looked guilty, and glanced at George. George frowned. She had told Mr Mandeville about the casket itself, and how they found it at the foot of the oak when the tree was struck by lightning, but so far she hadn't mentioned Johnson, or the young man pretending to be Benjamin Latchford. She quickly put things straight now – and Mr Mandeville himself seemed thunderstruck, like the oak tree!

'I'd never have believed it of Johnson!' he exclaimed. 'And to think how we trusted him! As for my nephew Benjamin – the real Benjamin – he's fair, not dark, and doesn't sound in the least like the young man you met. What's more, he's on holiday abroad at the moment!'

'Quick, let's go down to the cellar!' cried Dick. 'Coming, George?'

'We'll all go,' said Julian.

'So will I, if I may!' said Mr Mandeville.

Jenny went back to the kitchen, and a little procession set off down the cellar steps. George was leading the way – and the moment she entered the cellar she let out a cry. The old bedstead had been pushed aside, the sacks were scattered round the floor – and there was nothing else on the floor at all!

Julian, Dick, Anne and Tinker all exclaimed in horror too.

'The treasure's gone!'

'Woof!' agreed Timmy, running over to the sacks and sniffing them as he growled. Then he barked again. 'Woof, *woof*, WOOF!'

Mr Mandeville had turned very pale. 'Are you *quite* sure that's where you hid it?' he asked.

'Absolutely certain!' Julian told him. 'George took a lot of trouble to hide any traces that we'd been here, too!'

'And now,' said Dick, gloomily, 'anyone can see someone's been dragging the bedstead over the floor and scattering the sacks about without taking any precautions at all!'

George was standing perfectly still, thinking.

'I wonder how the thieves managed to get in here?' she murmured. 'This stone cellar is very old – Jenny told me it was part of the old hunting lodge that once stood here, and Rose Cottage was built on top of it. The door to the cellar steps is always locked, and Jenny keeps the key in a safe place. She had to go and fetch it for me when we hid the treasure here. And there's only one little window, high up in the wall, to let light into the cellar . . .'

Julian walked over to look at the window. 'That's closed, too, and looks as if it can't have been opened for centuries!' he said.

'The Mystery of the Locked Room!' said Anne,

who had once read a very exciting detective story with that title. 'Well – if nobody could come in or go out, how can the treasure have been stolen?'

Mr Mandeville too was checking the window and the door.

'*I* can't see any signs of a break-in,' he said, rather sternly. 'Are you really sure this is not a practical joke you've been playing on me?'

At that moment, Mischief dived into the dusty jumble of sacks. He picked up something shiny with his soft little paw, and held it out to Tinker.

'Oh, Mr Mandeville!' cried Tinker. 'Here's proof that we're not lying! Look! This jewel must have rolled out of the treasure casket. We've seen it before – a big, unset ruby! It's yours, sir – here you are!'

Mr Mandeville took the stone, put it in the hollow of his hand, and looked at it. It was translucent and deep red, with a wonderful pure glow.

'A ruby!' he murmured in amazement. 'One of the finest rubies I have ever seen! My dear young people – I am so sorry I ever doubted you! This certainly looks as if it proves the existence of the treasure. The thieves must have been quite dazzled by the contents of the casket if they let a wonderful jewel like this roll away, and never noticed!'

Meanwhile George had joined Timmy, who was still sniffing round the sacks, growling. She noticed several things, but she decided it would be better to keep quiet about them for the time being.

Mr Mandeville was already climbing up the steps out of the cellar. He went to find Jenny and tell her what had happened. Poor Jenny let out a cry of horror.

'Oh dear – oh, Mr Mandeville, whatever shall we do?'

'We must tell the police at once,' said Mr Mandeville. 'You come with me, children! We'll make a statement. You must tell the police the whole story, not forgetting that note signed with my name, and the visit from the young man pretending to be my nephew. Johnson is going to have some trouble proving his innocence!'

Down in the Cellar Again

Sure enough, as Mr Mandeville and the children had expected, the police immediately suspected Johnson. He was called to the police station – but he swore that he was innocent, he hadn't sent the note, he didn't know the fake 'Benjamin', and – so he said – he certainly knew nothing whatever about any burglary at Rose Cottage.

When the children and Mr Mandeville confronted him, he just stuck to his story, and said firmly, '*I don't know this dark haired lad with the motor-bike, however much you want to make out I'm in league with him. Never set eyes on him in my life! As for knowing about the discovery of the old treasure, why, that little girl –* ' and he pointed in a scornful way at poor Anne – '*that little girl was chattering away about it for anyone to hear! Anyone could have overheard her talking and tried to get hold of the treasure. I didn't believe a word of it, myself!*'

So it was impossible to prove that Johnson had written the note – especially as the children hadn't got it any more! That naughty little monkey Mischief had torn it up. The police had no solid evidence at all to back up their suspicions, so they had to let Johnson go home.

George, her cousins and Tinker were very disappointed. They were sure the man was guilty! Lunch at Rose Cottage that day was a dismal meal, and as soon as they had finished eating, the five friends held a council of war.

'I tell you what – we'd better make our own inquiries, in case the police don't get anywhere with theirs!' said George firmly. 'For a start, there are one or two things I'd like to show the rest of you. Let's go down to the cellar.'

The others followed her, wondering what she could mean. A little earlier, the police had been round for a brief look at the scene of the crime, and they had glanced at the cellar themselves, but they didn't seem to have been able to deduce much from anything there.

When they were all down the steps, George waved her hand round at the cellar. 'Right!' she said. 'Here's a good test of our powers of observation! Does anything in particular strike you about this burglary?'

'Yes, it does!' said Julian at once. 'None of the other rooms in the cottage were disturbed at all.

The thieves went straight to the cellar and took the treasure, just as if they already knew where to find it!'

'Well done, Julian! Good thinking!'

Anyone less good-natured than Julian might have been annoyed with his younger cousin for sounding a bit patronising, but he merely grinned and pretended to aim a blow at her!

'But apart from us and Jenny, nobody knew where the hiding place was!' Dick objected.

'Correct!' agreed George. 'So what do you deduce from *that*?'

'Well – the burglars must have begun their search of the house down in the cellar, and they struck lucky. They found the treasure straightaway!'

'That's what I'd have thought, too, if I hadn't taken a very close look,' said George, shaking her head. 'See those marks on the floor. Now, tell me what you make of them!'

Julian, Dick, Tinker and Anne looked at the marks left on the dusty floor by the bedstead and the sacks when they had been moved.

Rather surprisingly, Anne was the first to speak up – not that the little girl was at all stupid, but she did tend to be rather shy.

'That bedstead wasn't just dragged aside,' she remarked. 'It's been turned over first. And the sacks are scattered in a funny sort of way – as if they'd been pulled away from the wall into a kind of semicircle.'

'Not pulled away, exactly,' George told her cousin. '*Pushed* away!'

'Pushed away?' Dick looked at George blankly. 'What do you mean?'

'I mean the burglars weren't *facing* that end wall when they came into the cellar – they had it *behind* them!'

'But that's impossible!' cried Tinker. 'The only way in would have been that little window, and it's tiny, and tightly closed. They could never have got through it.'

'No, they didn't come through the window,' agreed George. '*Or* through the door, either!'

Julian looked at his cousin with interest. 'What are you getting at, George? Come on, spill the beans!'

'Well, those sacks lying in a semicircle, and the way the bedstead was upside down, as if something had knocked it over, all make me think the thieves came through a secret doorway in the end wall! And when they pushed the door open, they pushed away everything we'd piled in front of it. So then, there they were, face to face with the treasure which we'd so kindly put there for them. All they had to do was pick it up!'

'What an amazing coincidence that would be!' said Julian.

'Julian, my revered and respected cousin, life is *full* of amazing coincidences!' pronounced George, in a comically solemn tone. 'Anyway, we can check my theory!'

The five children scrambled over the bedstead, and began feeling the stones of the cellar wall. It was an unusually thick wall, the kind you sometimes see in very old buildings. Yes, it could easily be hiding a secret passage.

'And don't forget, this cellar is part of the old hunting lodge,' said George. 'Oh, I say – this stone seemed to move! If we all push together – '

Tinker was pushing so hard that when the stone pivoted on its own axis and swung aside, to reveal a dark, gaping hole, he almost fell into the hole head first.

'So I was right!' cried George, delighted. 'I know the country round here pretty well, you see – and almost all the old manor houses in these parts have underground passages like this one! I bet the other end comes out in the ruins of what used to be the Mandevilles' ancestral home. And it must pass close to Wisteria Lodge, too. I feel sure Johnson knows about it! Now, let's think. Nobody but Johnson knew the treasure was at Rose Cottage, so he must have come along the secret passage to get in and look for it – and he was lucky enough to find it straightaway! Oh dear, I could *kick* myself for thinking it would be such a good idea to hide

the suitcase containing the casket down here in
the cellar!'

'You weren't to know what would happen,' said
Julian, gloomily. 'But I rather think you're right,
George. Working for the Mandevilles, Johnson has
probably come to know the estate like the back of
his hand. And we've already worked out that he's
the only one who can have committed the crime,
knowing what he did know.'

'Gosh!' cried Dick excitedly. 'Listen, why don't
we go and get the treasure back? We can go the
same way as Johnson, only in the opposite direction.
Come on!'

'Not so fast, Dick! Calm down!' said Julian.
'Never mind the treasure now – we don't know
where he may have put it. But we *can* make a little
reconnaissance trip along this passage, for a start!'

Saying nothing to Jenny for fear of alarming her,
the children went to get their electric torches. Then
they climbed back down the cellar steps and into
the secret passage. Beyond the doorway made by
the pivoting stone, they found a staircase climbing
down underground. It led to a narrow passage of
solid masonry – luckily, though it must have gone
down quite deep, it was quite dry.

George was leading the way – and suddenly she
switched off her torch. The others followed suit
instinctively. 'Ssh!' she hissed. 'I thought I heard
something!'

They waited a few minutes, but nothing happened. It had been a false alarm. But as they stood there in the dark, the children realised they could see light ahead of them.

'Daylight!' whispered Anne. 'It must be the far end of the passage.'

They moved on again, taking even more precautions now. The floor of the passage was sloping upwards all the time at this point. Soon they reached the top of the slope – and saw the sun shining brightly through thickly intertwined branches just above their heads.

Cautiously, George peered out of the opening of the tunnel. When her eyes were at ground level, she let out a soft little cry of triumph.

'We're in the garden of Wisteria Lodge!' she whispered to her companions, who were standing perfectly still behind her. 'I can see the back of the house from here.'

So her theory had been correct. The secret passage *did* come out in the Mandevilles' garden, which had once been part of the grounds surrounding the old manor. But what should their next move be?

'What do we do now?' muttered Dick, echoing George's own thoughts. 'Shall we go and tell the Mandevilles what we've found – or what?'

'Wait a minute!' said George suddenly. 'Hm . . . that's funny! All the windows of Wisteria Lodge are closed – on this side of the house, at least!'

'Let's get a move on, anyway,' said Tinker. 'I'm stifling down in this hole!'

'We must go carefully, though,' George warned. 'We'll be in real trouble if we meet Johnson now!'

But the place seemed to be deserted. The children clambered up out of the underground passage. It ended in the middle of a thick hedge, and you'd never have seen it if you weren't looking for it. George guessed Johnson must have discovered it quite by chance while he was cutting the hedge, or something like that. Obviously even Mr Mandeville himself didn't know about it!

Very cautiously, the Five and Tinker went all round the house. But Wisteria Lodge was silent and shut up.

'The Mandevilles must have gone away again,' murmured Anne.

'Let's leave,' said Julian. 'We're trespassing, you know – I shan't feel happy until we're well away from here.'

All the five friends had to do was push open a little gate, which wasn't locked, and then they were out in the road. The cottage where, so Tinker had told them, Johnson lived was not far away.

'Why don't we try to find out if he's there?' suggested George. 'After all, if he's stolen the treasure, where can he be hiding it except in his own home?'

'This could be dangerous,' Julian warned the others.

'Nothing ventured, nothing gained!' said George.

'And fortune favours the bold!' added Dick, showing he could cap George's proverb and backing her up as usual.

The Five and Tinker went into the little garden behind Johnson's cottage, taking great care not to make any noise – and as they got closer they realised they could hear two men talking inside the little house.

'Johnson's at home!' whispered Tinker. 'And he's not alone, either!'

'Let's see if we can get a glimpse of him!' said Dick, going down on all fours and crawling over to the ground floor window from which the voices were coming. Then, slowly and cautiously, he raised his head to look in. 'I say!' he breathed. 'Look at that!'

The others followed him over to the window. It had taken them quite a long time to explore the cellar and go along the underground passage. The sun wasn't so hot now, and there were big clouds coming up to cover the sky. Looking into the room from outside, they had to peer hard to see anything, and as they didn't want to be seen themselves they had to be very, very careful too. But they could all make out the figures of two people. One was Johnson, and the other was the dark-haired young man who had pretended to be Benjamin Latchford. They were sitting at

the table with two bottles of beer in front of
them, talking quietly, with no idea that five pairs
of ears were listening most attentively to their
conversation!

— 8 —

An Interesting Conversation

'I'm surprised you didn't meet any of the police on your way here,' the caretaker of Wisteria Lodge was saying. 'They came to search the house not so long ago – but they left empty-handed, that's what matters! A real laugh, that was!'

'Acted all innocent and indignant, did you, Uncle Jim?' said the young man, laughing. 'I bet you had 'em puzzled! How were they to know you'd already got the goods safe away?'

'We've hit a winning streak all right, Gary!' said Johnson.

'Specially finding the treasure straight off like that, first go! Just think of those stupid kids hiding it down in the cellar, right in front of the secret door! And *what* a treasure, too!'

'When I opened up that rusty old box, you could have knocked me down with a feather!' agreed Johnson.

'The only thing is, Uncle Jim – well, all that gold and those jewels, they're kind of conspicuous! How are we going to get rid of them?'

'That'll be okay. Potter knows a man in London – what they call a fence. He'll be getting in touch with his friend. But there's no tearing hurry. Don't want to draw attention to ourselves, do we? We'll wait for the sensation to die down a bit. Meanwhile the loot's safe enough where it is. Well, here's to our success, Gary!'

The two men drank their beer, and then the younger one, Gary, left. The children could hear him starting his motorbike and riding off down the road.

They looked at each other. Well! They'd learnt a lot in a very short time! So the police had searched Johnson's house and found nothing. The young man who had pretended to be Benjamin was really the caretaker's nephew and was called Gary. He and his uncle were certainly guilty of stealing the treasure, and they had an accomplice called Potter. Moreover, George's theory about the way they used the underground passage had been right. And last but not least, Johnson planned to hand the gold and jewels over to a 'fence', who would get rid of them for him – but not just yet! That meant the Five and Tinker still had time to do something about it.

However, talkative as Johnson and his nephew had been, they hadn't been kind enough to mention the most important point: just *where* they had hidden the treasure!

When the sound of Gary's motorbike had died away, the children went back to Rose Cottage, wondering what to do next.

'I wish the Mandevilles hadn't gone away,' said Julian. 'But it does look as if they have, so let's hope they're back tomorrow. Then we must tell them what we've discovered!'

'Meanwhile, don't you think we ought to go to the police with our story?' asked Anne.

'What would be the use?' said George gloomily: 'All the police can do is question Johnson again, and he'll deny everything! What's more, it might make him decide to dispose of the treasure sooner then he planned at first, and get it away from here! No, that won't do at all. We must try to recover it ourselves. Why, for all we know it may actually be inside Wisteria Lodge itself! At any rate, Johnson can't have hidden it very far away. And I bet you he goes to look at it from time to time, to gloat over it and make sure it's still there in its hiding place. All we have to do is keep a close watch on him, and I think he'll lead us to it!'

Dick agreed with his cousin, and Julian decided, 'All right, then, that's what we'll do. We'll take turns keeping watch on Johnson, starting tomorrow!'

Next morning Jenny went out shopping very

early, and came back with some news that interested
the children a great deal. The post-mistress had
told her that Mr Mandeville had been unexpectedly
called back to London on urgent business the day
before, and as his wife didn't like being left alone
in the house she had gone with him, but they both
expected to be back soon.

George, her cousins and Tinker exchanged meaning glances as Jenny told them this. If Johnson's
employers were away, he'd be free to visit his
treasure in Wisteria Lodge – that is, if he really
had hidden it there! In any case he'd be more likely
to move about without taking so many precautions,
and that might well make things easier for the
children.

They immediately drew up a rota for following
Johnson. They intended to take turns keeping an
eye on him the whole time, except at night – from
what he'd been saying to Gary, they didn't think he
planned to move the treasure yet, so they needn't
keep a watch on him all round the clock at this point.
During the day, however, somebody would be near
him, even at mealtimes.

Disappointingly, however, Johnson's daily life
turned out to be very dull! He didn't go out much
at all, except to work in the garden of Wisteria
Lodge or to do a little shopping. And this went
on for two days.

'You know, I'm beginning to think he's got the

treasure hidden in his own cottage after all,' George said, several times. 'I know the police searched it and didn't find anything, but he may have a very good hiding place there.'

And in the end Julian, Dick, Anne and Tinker came round to George's point of view. It was true that Johnson hardly ever left his cottage – he was like a dog jealously guarding a bone!

'Well, we can't go on like this!' said George, on the third day. 'We must *do* something! Next time that horrible man goes out, let's go and search his cottage ourselves. After all, he can hardly complain of *us* breaking in – that's just what *he* did!'

Julian wasn't at all sure that this was a good idea, but the others all agreed with George, so in the end he had to give way.

And they got their chance that very afternoon! Johnson went off to Wisteria Lodge to mow the lawns. The children went straight to his cottage, thinking they would have plenty of time to look round.

As it turned out, getting into the house was quite easy, because one of the ground floor windows at the back had been left open. They quickly searched the cottage, but they didn't find anything.

Dick sighed. 'Just what we might have expected, I suppose!' he said. 'If the police didn't find anything, we couldn't really hope to have better luck!'

'No, and the police must have had a search

warrant too, which is more than we've got!' said Julian. 'Come on, you've had your way, George, and now we'd better clear out!'

'Oh, Ju, I'm *sure* the treasure can't be far away!' George protested. 'There are a couple of little out-buildings – let's search those before we go, and see if – '

But Anne interrupted her. 'Ssh!' she hissed: She was looking very frightened. 'Oh dear – I can hear footsteps. It must be Johnson, coming back!'

Glancing quickly round to make sure no trace of their presence in the cottage was left behind, the children scrambled out of the window again. Timmy had run on ahead, and they retreated without a sound. Only just in time! Anne was right – Johnson was coming home.

On the way back to Rose Cottage they stopped in a meadow, under a shady oak tree, to get their breath back.

'We mustn't give up hope,' said George. 'We'll go on searching tomorrow if we can. Don't forget, Johnson's cottage is on the Manor grounds too – and for all we know the whole place is riddled with underground passages. Maybe there's another one somewhere close, and Johnson has hidden his loot there!'

Luck was with the children again next day. Johnson went back to Wisteria Lodge to cut the hedges. The five friends didn't go into the cottage

itself today, and that set Julian's mind more at
rest! Instead, they searched the garden and the
yard. There was a sort of toolshed without a front
wall, so it was open to all weathers, and nothing
much of value could be stored in there. But then
George's attention was attracted by another little
structure built in the yard – an old stone washing
trough with a roof over it to shelter it and a little
raised stone wall round it. It was the sort of thing
that would have been used for a huge family wash
in the old days, and the bottom of the trough itself
was paved with several big flagstones. Followed
by Timmy, George prowled round the structure,
examining every stone. She soon found that one
stone stuck out a little farther than the others, and
she called to her companions.

'Hey, come over here, will you? I'd like to try
moving this stone!'

Julian and Dick hurried over to lend her a hand –
and they found they could lift the stone right out of
place. A kind of rusty handle came into view behind
it. Julian pulled the handle, and one of the big stones
paving the trough began moving aside! George had
suspected another underground passage might exist
– and it looked as if this could be the way into it!

'What did I tell you?' she cried, delighted, and
she plunged straight into the dark hole under the
stone. 'Come on! What a good thing we've got our
torches with us!'

The other children followed her. Julian brought up the rear. He wanted to make sure that once he'd put the flagstone back in place, he could move it easily from underneath, and to his great satisfaction he found there was a lever inside the tunnel which was obviously meant to do the job. He was just using it to close the opening when he let out a soft exclamation. Heavy footsteps were approaching! Johnson must be back earlier than they'd have expected again – he certainly wasn't keen to leave his cottage for any length of time. He had just come into the garden, and was walking towards the big trough!

'Watch out!' whispered Julian, manoeuvring the flagstone back into place in a hurry. 'Johnson's back already. I don't think he's spotted us, but it was a close thing! Let's hope *he's* not going to come down here too.'

They daren't hang about. There was nowhere the children *could* go but straight ahead, and if they were out of luck and Johnson followed them into the passage, they'd have to find a hiding place as fast as they could and hope he wouldn't discover them.

Anne's heart was beating fast as she followed her intrepid cousin George along the underground passage. Tinker and Dick were just behind her, and Julian came last. George had advised the others not to use their torches – they didn't want the least little bit of light to show if there were any openings along the way. She kept only her own, small torch switched on, and as they moved forward she shone its narrow, golden beam down on the ground ahead of her.

— 9 —

Adventure Underground

The floor of the underground tunnel was uneven, and the children kept stumbling. Suddenly the passage turned a corner, and they stopped to listen.

'It's all right. I can't hear anything,' whispered George.

But Timmy had pricked up his ears. He was whining very quietly, as if to tell her she was wrong. The children listened harder, and they thought they heard a sound behind them.

'I think it's Johnson moving the flagstone away!' whispered Tinker.

'Come on, quick!' Julian gave his brother a little shove. George had already started to hurry forward, and was helping Anne along. This was a risky situation! If Johnson found them down here he might not actually hurt them, though they couldn't be sure of that, but it would be a disaster all the same. He'd be very suspicious, and would probably move the treasure somewhere farther away at once. He might even decide to run for it earlier than he'd planned, taking his haul with him.

Timmy was going ahead now, sniffing the ground, his sensitive nose twitching. The children could hear Johnson's heavy footsteps coming closer behind them. The caretaker probably knew this place inside out, and he was going faster than they were. He'd catch up with them before very long!

Suddenly the children stopped short. They had come out in a little, round, underground cavern. Fallen rocks littered the floor. The passage obviously went on beyond this cavern, but there was a grating over its mouth to stop anyone getting into it. The children were caught in a trap!

Timmy whined again, and Anne bit back a cry of terror. Dick, Julian and Tinker looked frantically round. Then George, who was keeping quite cool, saw a heap of old sacks thrown carelessly into a corner.

'Quick!' she said. 'Let's hide under those!'

They hurried over to the sacks. George made Timmy lie down and covered him up. Then she and the others slipped under the sacks too and waited there, motionless and huddling together, hardly daring to breathe. George had switched her torch off, of course, so it was pitch dark. Mischief snuggled close to Tinker, and kept as still as his master.

They could hear Johnson's footsteps quite clearly now – and they could make out the faint light of a lantern as they peered through the coarse sacking.

'Oh, I do hope he doesn't look this way!' thought Anne to herself.

She needn't have worried. Even if Johnson *had* looked in their direction he couldn't have told there was anyone there. The children were quite invisible in their hiding place in such dim light. Johnson went up to the grating – and thinking he was alone, he began talking to himself out loud. He sounded very cheerful indeed.

'A nice fit, this little grating!' he said. 'The door to Jim Johnson's private safe, eh? Ha, ha! ha!'

Julian and his companions heard a slight click, and they realised that the caretaker of Wisteria Lodge must be opening up the grating. Then there was a very faint squealing sound, not at all loud. They guessed Johnson had been careful to give the hinges of the door of his 'safe' plenty of oil!

George ventured to lift one corner of a sack and look out of her hiding place. She could see Johnson's back. The grating was open now, and he was moving on along the tunnel, carrying his lantern.

'Now what?' whispered Dick, who was just behind her. 'Shall we go back down the passage and get out that way?'

'No,' said Julian at once. 'Johnson's still too close – he might easily hear us!'

'Listen,' said George softly. 'I've an idea he's gone to take a look at the treasure – so let's stay here till he leaves again, and then we can go on the same way he went and recover our property, or rather, Mr Mandeville's property. That's what we came for, isn't it?'

The children had to wait patiently for quite a long time, but at last Johnson came back. He seemed to be in a very good mood, and was chuckling away like an old hen cackling!

'Ho, ho – those lovely gold coins!' he muttered, closing the grating. 'Wonder what they'll fetch? Whatever it is, Jim Johnson's going to be a rich man – ha, ha, ha!'

His chuckling died away as he went back along the part of the underground passage that ended in the old washing trough in his cottage yard.

'Did you hear what he said?' asked George, triumphantly. 'I was right! The treasure's some-where here, quite close. All we have to do is go and get it!'

Quickly, the children threw off the sacks which had done such a good job of hiding them. Timmy jumped about to get the circulation in his paws going again. George hurried over to the grating. She took it in both hands and shook it, but it wouldn't budge.

'Oh, bother!' she said.

'Half a sec!' said Julian, 'There's no lock, so that means there must be a lever or a secret spring or something to work the mechanism, if we can just find it.'

In the end it was Anne's nimble fingers that found the little knob to open the grating. All you had to do was press it, hard, and the grating swung open with that slight squeal the children had heard before. They felt jubilant!

It turned out that the passage didn't go much farther beyond the grating. Instead, they came to a sudden opening. They were on the edge of a circular well! Or rather, as they realised in a minute or so, when they had got their bearings, they were about half-way down the well-shaft. It extended above and below them, and they saw the gleam of water a couple of feet down. There was no way to go on – only up or down!

'Well, this means that Johnson must have hidden the treasure somewhere along this last short stretch of the tunnel,' said Dick happily. 'It shouldn't take us long to search the place thoroughly. Come on!'

However, the children were in for a disappointment. Hard as they searched every nook and cranny of the underground passage, there was no sign of the suitcase containing the casket, or the casket itself. The treasure didn't seem to be anywhere here.

'What a nuisance!' said Julian. 'I just can't make it out!'

And then, for the third time, the children heard a now familiar sound.

'Oh no!' cried Dick. 'That grating's swinging shut again! We ought to have wedged it open with something!'

They all ran back, but they were just too late to catch the grating and hold it open. It closed right in their faces, with a dry click.

'Just our luck!' exclaimed Tinker. 'We're prisoners here now!'

'Well, all we have to do is press the knob that works the grating,' Dick pointed out. But that was easier said than done. The knob was in the underground cavern on the other side of the grating – and it was out of reach! Julian was the biggest of the children, and had the longest arms, but though he tried putting his arm through the bars he still couldn't touch the knob.

Then Tinker thought of making Mischief slip out through the bars to get at the knob. Mischief could do that all right, and he tried to obey Tinker's signs that he was to press the knob, but unfortunately he wasn't strong enough to push it right in hard. He did his best, but the grating stayed closed. At their wits' end, the children tried to tear it down, all together, but that was no use either.

'Well, there's no point in exhausting ourselves struggling with this stupid grating!' said George. 'Why don't we go back to the well and see if we can find some other way out?'

George, Julian and Dick were all being very calm

and brave, and but for that Anne and Tinker might have been even more frightened than they were. For they were in a very unpleasant situation, trapped underground! And as nobody knew where they had gone, they couldn't hope for any help to arrive.

However, George marched back to the well with determination. Leaning over, she shone her torch inside. She couldn't tell how deep the water at the bottom was, but obviously they couldn't get out that way. Next she shone her torch up, but she could see nothing at all. She switched the torch off, but went on looking up, and when her eyes got used to the dark she could make out a faint circle of light overhead. But not too far overhead!

'Good!' she said. 'It's not so very far up to the top of this well-shaft, and though I think there's a round lid over it, so long as the lid can be moved from inside we'll be all right if we can hoist ourselves up there! I bet we can get out that way!'

'But how can we ever climb that far?' asked Tinker. He sounded worried.

George switched her torch on again and shone it round the sides of the well. She gave a cry of triumph. 'Look – I thought there'd be something of this kind! Iron rungs set in the wall to make a sort of ladder. Quick, let's go up!'

'Oh no!' cried Anne. 'I can't! I'd be too scared!'

'You'll be much more scared if you stay down this well!' said George briskly.

'Wait a minute,' said Julian, stretching his arm out to take hold of a rung and put all the weight he could on it. 'We've got to make sure it's safe first!'

But it turned out that all the iron rungs were firmly fixed in the side of the well. George insisted on going first, and the others all watched anxiously as she climbed up. She soon reached the top of the well. With a heave of her shoulder, she tried raising the circular wooden lid, and to everyone's relief it came away easily. George stepped out into broad daylight.

A glance round her told her just where she was – at the bottom of the garden of Wisteria Lodge, not very far from the tangled hedge which hid the end of the other underground passage!

Leaning over the side of the well, she called down, quietly, 'Dick! Tinker! Anne! Come on up – hurry! Ju, do you mind waiting a bit? I must go and look for a rope, so we can haul Timmy up.'

While Anne and the two younger boys climbed out of the well, George ran to the tool shed in the garden of Wisteria Lodge, and was lucky enough to find a length of good strong cord, which would do for pulling Timmy up. She went back to the well and let one end of the cord down to Julian. He wrapped his jacket round the dog, then tied the cord round him, and a moment later George and Dick were hauling away. Up went Timmy, like a passenger in a balloon!

Then Julian too climbed out of the well, and they put the lid back on top. Now all they had to do was go back to Rose Cottage, though they put the cord they had borrowed back in the toolshed first.

However, they still hadn't found the treasure, and next day they decided to go in search of it again. As it certainly hadn't been in the part of the underground passage they had searched so thoroughly, they deduced that it might be actually inside the well itself, or at least somewhere very near it.

Julian was not quite happy about this expedition, and kept saying they must take great care, but George was determined to climb back down the well and see if there was anything at the bottom.

The children thought it would be a good idea to wait until dusk until they set out to explore the well – they didn't want Johnson to find them at it, and he might well be working in the garden of Wisteria Lodge again during the day. Directly after supper, however, they got their bicycles out and told Jenny they were going for a ride.

They reached Wisteria Lodge, got into the garden through the little side gate, and made straight for the well. They had brought their torches, and a length of good stout rope. Julian insisted on George's tying it round her waist before she climbed down the iron rungs inside the well.

'And we'll tie the other end to this tree,' he said.

'Then if you do happen to slip, we can soon haul you up again!'

So George tied the rope round herself, and began climbing down. Once she had reached the level of the water down below, she got a stone out of her pocket. It had a hole in the middle, and she had tied it to a piece of thin string. She let the stone down into the water, and found that it very soon touched bottom. George fished it out again, and now she could tell how deep the water was by looking at the wet part of the string.

'Good!' she called up to her cousins, who were leaning over the edge. 'The water's not at all deep. Now, I wonder . . .'

As she spoke, she was shining her torch round the walls of the well that surrounded her. An idea had suddenly come into her head! Suppose Johnson had hidden the treasure *underwater*?

Suddenly a gleam came into her eyes. She had just spotted a cord tied to the bottom iron rung, and hanging down into the water. She pulled it with her free hand, and soon a package came in sight. A heavyweight plastic bag, wrapped round a rusty old casket – the casket containing the treasure! She recognised it at once through the transparent plastic.

George let out a shout of triumph! 'I've got the treasure!' she called. 'It's here! I'm coming up again!'

As she fastened the cord tied to the casket to the rope she was wearing, Julian, Dick, Anne and Tinker all called down their congratulations, but quietly, because they didn't want to be heard. However, their excitement infected Timmy too. He bounded forward to the edge of the well, and as *he* didn't mind how much noise he made, he started barking at George, who was just coming up. The weight of the treasure slowed her down. Tinker raised his hand to give Timmy a tiny little tap, just to make him stop barking, but Timmy swerved to avoid it – and lost his balance!

The poor dog tumbled down the well just as his mistress was emerging into the open. George wasted no time in going to the rescue. Quickly, she untied the casket which she had brought up the well, dumped it in Dick's hands, and then climbed down again as fast as she could. Down below, poor Timmy had hit the water with a mighty splash, but he was up above the surface again by now, dog-paddling round and round with a lot of spluttering.

'Don't worry, Timmy! I'm coming!' she called.

She was soon within reach of Timmy. 'Gosh, we *are* having what you might call a ropy sort of evening!' she muttered, as she grabbed him by the collar. Undoing the rope Julian had made her wear, she tied it round Timmy, with some difficulty.

'Ready up there?' she shouted. 'Haul Timmy up, then!'

The rescue operation was carried out in complete silence. Then George came up again too – and almost fell back in, in her surprise at the sight that met her eyes!

Timmy was safe and sound all right, busy shaking himself. But Julian, Dick, Anne and Tinker were standing perfectly still, looking rather pale and scared. Johnson the caretaker was facing them, aiming a shotgun at them, while his nephew Gary investigated the plastic bag to make sure the treasure was still there!

Prisoners

So that was why everything had suddenly gone so quiet during Timmy's rescue! The children had fallen right into their enemies' hands.

George immediately realised that they were in a tight spot. Johnson and Gary had been unmasked – they couldn't pretend to be innocent any longer. The discovery of the treasure proved their guilt. And now they'd got it back again!

'They'll never let us go!' thought George, with a shiver. 'We'd be much too dangerous as witnesses.'

Julian exchanged a despairing glance with his cousin. *He* was thinking much the same thing too. 'What will they do with us now?' he wondered.

Far too late in the day, George was wishing she hadn't been quite so daring. *She* was the one who'd led the others into this mess. Getting over his fright, Timmy suddenly began growling.

'Quiet, Timmy!' George ordered, terrified in

case Johnson shot her beloved dog to keep him quiet.

The good dog obeyed her, and the five children pressed close together as they faced their enemies.

'It's okay!' said Gary, straightening up. 'They didn't get time to open the bag. Well, Uncle Jim, what do we do with these kids now? Can't let 'em go, can we?'

'No, we can't,' agreed Johnson, frowning. 'Wretched brats – what a pest! We'll have to change our plans and get them out of the way, if we want room to move freely.'

'Keep them prisoner, you mean? Or what?'

Anne began to cry, quietly. Dick smiled at her to encourage her. 'Cheer up, Anne,' he whispered. 'They're thieves, but not murderers!'

George looked at her cousins and Tinker. 'I say – I'm awfully sorry I dragged all of you into this!' she said, with her usual straightforward honesty.

'You kids shut up!' Johnson told them roughly. 'I've got to think what to do about you!'

Keeping his gun pointed at them, the caretaker began talking to his nephew. They had lowered their voices, but it was a still night, and the children could hear most of what they said.

'We might do best to clear out straightaway,' suggested Gary.

'Can't do that – we've got to wait for Potter to

come back, bringing word from his London friend, and that'll be another couple of days yet!'

'But meanwhile what'll these kids be up to? If we let 'em go, they'll make a beeline for the police and tell them all they know!'

'We'll have to keep them somewhere,' grunted Johnson.

'Yes, but where? Not in your cottage – much too risky, and the police may search it again. The same goes for Wistaria Lodge, even if the Mandevilles don't come home – and they could, any time!'

Gary stopped to think for a moment. Suddenly he uttered a triumphant exclamation.

'I know, Uncle Jim! I was riding my motorbike round the place one day when I spotted a little island off the coast. It's a small place, and uninhabited – that's the bit that makes it so suitable! I reckon nobody ever sets foot there. It's got some ramshackle old ruins on it, and that's all! We can take these nosy parkers over and leave 'em on the island, with a few blankets and some food. When Potter arrives, we'll be off – leaving a message behind to say where the kids can be found. How about that?'

Johnson thought his nephew's idea was a good one. 'Let's get a move on, then!' he said. 'I'll get the Mandevilles' motor-boat out. Come on, you kids!'

Julian reluctantly obeyed – there was nothing else to be done. Dick gritted his teeth. Tinker and Anne were holding hands as if to cheer each other up, and Mischief was huddling close to his master. But George, one hand on Timmy's collar, stepped briskly forward with a funny little smile on her lips. Suddenly, Johnson stopped.

'I've been thinking!' he told Gary. 'We don't want to work too fast, and maybe do something stupid. There are more precautions we ought to take – let's go into the greenhouse and talk things over.'

So Gary shepherded the children into the greenhouse. His uncle was no fool – Johnson had thought of several details that might spoil his plans, as he now explained. First, once she realised the children were missing, Professor Hayling's housekeeper was bound to worry. Jenny would raise the alarm!

'So we must make her think everything's okay,' the caretaker said. 'Otherwise she'll go to the police and the kids' parents! But I have a plan. Gary, take this cord and tie our prisoners' hands behind their backs – yes, that'll do!'

Gary carried out this task very efficiently, while Johnson kept the gun aimed at his prisoners. George and the others felt furious, but they had to stand still and let Gary tie their wrists together. When all five of them were helpless, the caretaker at last lowered his gun.

'Right!' he said. 'Now, you wait here for me and guard them, Gary. I won't be long!'

'What are you going to do?'

'Run back to my cottage as fast as I can. I'll phone

that housekeeper, what's her name – Jenny – and make out I'm Mr Kirrin telephoning from Kirrin Cottage!'

George bit her lip. Johnson was very crafty! He'd obviously taken the trouble to find out just who they were and where they came from.

'You're crazy!' exclaimed Gary. 'The old girl must know Mr Kirrin's voice – you'll never be able to fool her!'

'Oh yes, I will! I'll talk in a hoarse tone, making out I've got a cold. I won't speak to her for long, either, just say the kids have gone over to Kirrin Cottage and I'm keeping them there a couple of days, so she's not to worry!'

'Good thinking, Uncle Jim! Well done!' said Gary admiringly.

The children exchanged miserable glances. They felt cut off from the rest of the world in this dark greenhouse, lit up only by their captors' torches. 'That awful Johnson has thought of everything!' George told herself. 'And Jenny's so trusting, she'll swallow his story and never suspect! Oh, how I wish I hadn't been so careless!'

Johnson wasn't gone long. 'That went off very well!' he told his nephew, smiling. 'Now, follow me, you lot! I've got the boat out.'

'You haven't brought any food or blankets for them,' Gary pointed out.

'I've thought better of that! They can do without.

I told you just now I'd been thinking – well, one thing that struck me is this island of yours may be deserted, but who's to say tourists don't land on it to picnic there? So if we leave the kids loose, they'll only have to tell their story to anyone who happens by, get brought back to the mainland, and then we'll be in real trouble! No, I've got a better notion. You told me there are some old ruins – there's sure to be a cellar or suchlike there. Old places like that always had cellars.'

'It was a castle, I think,' said Gary. 'Could be there are dungeons.'

'Even better! Well, we'll find somewhere in the ruins to leave our young friends shut up – they'll have shelter there from the night air, and as for food and drink, a forty-eight hours' starvation diet won't hurt 'em – ha, ha! Come on, kids, start moving!'

As George had told herself, Johnson really *had* thought of everything – and yet she was still smiling in a mysterious way, although the other children were looking very downcast.

Johnson and Gary took the children down to the beach, where the Mandevilles' boathouse stood, and made them get into Mr Mandeville's motor launch. Gary started the engine. George noticed which way he was going, and began to smile again. Just as she'd thought!

Dick noticed her smile, but he was sensible enough not to ask any questions. And sad to say, it was soon to be wiped off her face anyway – because when Gary thought he was far enough out from shore, he bent down and without any warning took hold of Timmy and threw him into the water. Then, before the children had even recovered from their amazement, he snatched Mischief away from Tinker and threw him into the sea too, after Timmy!

'You brute!' cried George, in horror. 'Get my dog out again – you can't do a thing like that!'

Tinker was shouting indignantly too, but Gary just laughed.

'Can't I just! That dog might give away the place we're going to hide you in by barking – and for all we know, the monkey may be well trained enough to untie you. I hope the nasty creatures drown!'

Well, George knew that Timmy wouldn't do that – he was a good swimmer, and could easily get back to the shore, and Mischief was intelligent enough to cling to his stronger friend. But she didn't want her dog to tire himself out by following the boat – and that was just what he was doing! Seeing him swim after them, Johnson threatened him with an oar. In the moonlight, George saw Timmy give her a sad look, and then he swam away. Her eyes filled with tears. This was one of the very few times her cousins had ever seen her cry!

A few moments later the boat came ashore on the island Gary had seen from his motorbike – and now the others knew why George had been smiling so mysteriously as they boarded the boat! It was none other than Kirrin Island, George's very own property, where the Five had often been to camp!

Of course George had guessed at once where they were being taken. She knew the local countryside inside out, and there weren't any *other* uninhabited islands close to Kirrin. Julian, Dick, Anne and Tinker were feeling a little better now they were on familiar ground. As for the dungeons where the crooks planned to shut them up – well, those dungeons held no terrors for the Five.

'Come on, move! Faster!' growled Johnson. 'My word, this path's steep!' he added to his nephew. 'Ah – there are those ruins of yours!'

Uncle and nephew had to search about for a few minutes before they found the way down to the dungeons. George had a mad impulse to call out and tell them where to look, but she restrained herself! At last Johnson moved aside the stone over the entrance. 'Here we are!' he cried. Then he shone his torch down the dark way into the dungeons, and said roughly, 'In you go, kids! Two days in the dark with your hands tied, waiting for someone to come and let you out, and without anything to eat – that'll cure you of wanting to poke your noses into other folks' business! Come on, Gary! Let's go! I tell you what – I've just had another idea too. We'll leave the treasure on this island as well, buried in the castle courtyard. There couldn't be a safer place for it! And when Potter's back, tomorrow or the day after, we'll come over to collect our property!'

— 11 —

On Kirrin Island

The two criminals went off, taking no more notice of their prisoners. 'Well, what a couple of idiots!' laughed Dick, when they were out of earshot. 'They were afraid *Timmy* would bark, but they forgot to gag *us*! And they must have thought we were deaf or something, talking about the treasure so freely in front of us!'

'They know we can't get out of here,' Tinker pointed out. 'I'm tied up so tight my arms feel numb already.'

George was still furious with the men for the way they'd treated Timmy, and she certainly wasn't going to admit herself beaten, not on her own island! 'Who says we can't get out of here?' she asked. 'You saw what they did to Timmy and Mischief – well, they're not getting away with that! And this is *my* island! I bet you the stones of these ruins themselves will help us!'

She was making her way over to one of the dungeon walls. When she got there, she turned her back to the wall and began rubbing the cord that tied her hands against the rough stones. She hurt her hands, but she didn't mind that. She just *had* to get free!

Following her example, the other children tried rubbing through their bonds. It took ages – but at last they did it. George and Julian were free first, and they helped Dick, Anne and Tinker. Then they all went back the way they had come, and soon they were back at the stone which hid the entrance to the dungeons. They all pushed together, and it swung aside. They were free!

The children ran out into the open. Day was already dawning in the east, over the mainland. Suddenly George let out a cry of delight.

'Look – it's Timmy! Timmy's swimming out to join us!'

She was right. Under the golden rays of the rising sun, they could see the good dog swimming bravely through the waves. And he wasn't alone! Mischief, clinging to his neck, was having a ride on his back. It was Tinker's turn to shout with glee now.

'Mischief! Timmy's brought Mischief with him!'

The children began dancing and jumping for joy. A moment later, Timmy and his 'rider' were shaking themselves on the beach. The dog bounded up to George and began licking her face.

'Timmy dear, you've come at just the right moment. Now you can help us – and get your revenge on those horrible men for throwing you into the sea!' she said.

Tinker and Mischief were dancing about on the sand. Julian, Dick and Anne were laughing at the sight, forgetting how scared they had been not so long ago.

'And there's something else we must do,' cried Dick suddenly. 'Come on, let's hurry – we must get the treasure back!'

That was not very difficult. They hurried off to the castle courtyard, and Julian soon spotted a piece of ground which looked as if it had been dug quite recently. It was rather clumsily covered with three big stones. The children found a stick to dig with, and they soon unearthed the casket of treasure.

'Let's hide it in our larder,' suggested George. 'We can't be too careful!'

The 'larder' was a useful secret recess in one of the ruined castle walls, where she always kept reserve supplies of tinned food, sugar and salt, and other provisions that wouldn't go bad and that the children could use when they came to camp on the island. George liked a bit of mystery, and had hidden her provisions as carefully as if they were treasure. So the real treasure would feel quite at home in its improvised safe, and the emergency provisions were going to come in very useful!

Now the five friends were holding all the trump cards! They had escaped from their dark prison, they had recovered the treasure, and they were on their own home ground again.

'George, how do you think we can get our own back on those dreadful men?' Anne asked her cousin.

'We'll discuss that in a minute,' said George. 'But first let's have some breakfast! I'm starving. There's tinned milk, chocolate, and cocoa powder in the larder. No bread, but we've got plenty of biscuits! Get the little spirit stove out, Dick – and you run off and fetch some water from the spring, Tinker!'

It was rather a funny breakfast, but it tasted wonderful. The children felt much better with some food and hot cocoa inside them. After their meal, they talked the situation over.

'There's no problem about staying on the island,' said Julian. 'We can perfectly well camp out here until Johnson and his friends come back – we've often camped here before, so we shan't feel marooned at all! I wish we could get a message to Uncle Quentin, though.'

'Well, so we can!' said George. 'I'm a very strong swimmer. I can easily swim over to the mainland and raise the alarm.'

'Oh no, you don't!' said Julian firmly. 'This may be *your* island, George, but *I'm* the eldest, and I say you're not to do anything so dangerous. It would be rash and stupid!'

George knew he was right, really. She went rather pink in the face, and shook her head. 'Oh, very well, if you say so!' she agreed. 'But anyway,' she added, with a slightly mischievous smile, 'that wasn't what I'd actually planned to do! We can deal with those men ourselves, you know – we don't need help.'

'How do you mean?' asked Tinker, his eyes shining.

'Well, here's what I've been thinking. When Johnson, Gary and their friend Potter get here, we'll have all sorts of booby-traps waiting! They won't be expecting anything like that, and I bet we can drive them off that way – and into the hands of the police. So now, let's start thinking of some really good booby-traps!'

Dick burst out laughing. 'Good idea, George!' he said. 'Ha, ha! Those men don't know what's coming to them!'

'And we'll have the advantage of surprise on our side,' Julian pointed out. 'They won't know we're free – they'll think we're still tied up in the dungeons.'

'They don't know Timmy and Mischief are safe and sound and have joined us, either,' added Tinker.

'*Or* that they've lost the treasure!' said Anne happily, smiling.

'Now to draw up a plan of action, then,' said George. 'We must keep careful watch, taking turns. We don't want *them* taking *us* by surprise when they come back.'

So the five friends spent most of the morning working out what Dick described as their 'anti-Johnson strategy'. Then they made themselves lunch from the reserve supplies. What a good thing George had laid in plenty of tins of baked beans and sausages at the very beginning of the holidays! There were tinned peaches too, and Anne found a packet of lemonade crystals in the 'larder' and made lemonade with the fresh spring water – delicious! After their meal, they went on with their planning, preparing a fine reception for Johnson, his nephew, and their accomplice Potter.

When dark fell that night, they fetched the old blankets that they always kept in the only room in the castle that still had a roof on it. The blankets stayed nice and dry in there. The children rolled up in them and went to sleep. It wasn't by any means the first time they'd slept in the ruins of the castle – they didn't have their sleeping bags, as usual, but it was quite a mild night.

George took the first night watch. She sat at the top of the path which led down to the little beach for two hours, with Timmy beside her, watching the sea. Then Dick relieved her. After that it was Julian's turn, then Tinker's, and finally Anne took over at dawn. But the thieves did not appear. The children went on keeping watch until evening – they felt sure it wouldn't be long before Johnson and the others came back now.

In fact, it was exactly nine o'clock that evening, and dusk was falling, when Tinker, who was on watch at the time, called out to the others.

'Here we are!' he cried. 'I can see a motor-boat making this way!'

'I'm sure that's them!' cried George, getting very excited. 'Good! Come on, then – and find out what's waiting for you!'

The Treasure is Safe

Yes, it was Johnson, Gary, and Potter all right! Lying flat on their stomachs on top of the cliff, the children saw them get out of the boat. It was getting dark quite fast now, but the moon was rising, so they had quite enough light to see by. Potter was a stocky, rough looking man.

'Okay, then!' he told his companions in a hoarse voice. 'If this is where you left that treasure, better get it back quick, ready to hand over to the fence, Tracy. He's expecting us tomorrow, remember!'

'I'll go ahead with a torch,' said Gary. 'By the way, what are we going to do with those kids? I don't suppose *they'll* be feeling very chirpy after two days down there in the dark!'

'Them?' said Johnson, callously. 'Oh, a phone call to their parents once we're in London will do! Interfering brats – serves 'em right for all the trouble they've given us!'

'And we're going to give you some more trouble, too!' muttered George between her teeth. 'For a start, take this!'

With a perfectly steady hand, she neatly tossed a pebble over the cliff. It fell – and hit Johnson, down below, right on the head.

'Ouch!' cried Johnson, putting a hand on the crown of his head. 'What was that?'

'Only a pebble falling off the cliff-top,' said Gary. 'Don't make such a fuss, Uncle Jim!'

At that very moment, he himself fell heavily to the ground. The shock of the fall broke the glass of his torch into tiny pieces.

'What's up with *you*?' said Johnson. 'Can't you keep your footing?'

'I slipped on something,' grunted Gary. 'Goodness knows what!'

Dick could have told him! He was the one who had carefully poured the contents of a whole bottle of cooking oil over the stony surface of the path. It made a big, slippery puddle – it was not surprising Gary had slipped and fallen!

He got up – and then it was Johnson's turn to go sprawling. When Potter came over to help him up, *he* slipped too. Gary stood there laughing at the pair of them. 'So you two can't stay on your feet either!' he said.

Cursing, the two men scrambled up, and made their way up the steep path, slipping and sliding wherever Dick had poured the oil. Meanwhile the children, Timmy and Mischief had set off for the castle again. Soon the three crooks reached the courtyard.

'It's over here!' said Johnson, stopping beside the spot where he had buried the casket containing the treasure. 'Dig here, Gary!'

Gary moved the stones, and began scraping away the crumbly earth with his bare hands.

'Here it is!' he announced happily, digging up a plastic bag. 'Now – just take a look at this, Potter!'

Potter took the bag, put his big hand inside, and brought out the casket. Eyes gleaming with greed, he opened it – and let out a cry of disgust. Instead of the gold and jewels he was expecting to find, he was looking at the skeleton of a large seagull which the children had found on the beach. They had put it in the casket and filled up the space with pebbles.

'Is *this* your treasure?' he shouted angrily.

The astonished Johnson raised his torch for a better look – but as he did so it was snatched away from him by a strange little creature which seemed to have appeared out of nowhere, and which ran off towards the castle doorway with the torch.

'What was that?' shouted the caretaker. 'It looked like a monkey – but how could there be a monkey here? Catch it, Gary!'

Gary set off after Mischief the monkey as fast as

he could go. Mischief kept stopping, as if to wait for him, and then running on again – he was leading Gary into the ruins.

The young man ran after him – and stumbled over a string stretched across the doorway. Carried on by his own impetus, he fell head first, knocked his head on a big rock, and lost consciousness.

Silently, the children emerged from the shadows where they had been hiding. They picked Gary up, carried him away, and put him down out of sight behind a wall.

Johnson and Potter, who were still outside the ruins, heard a miserable voice, amplified by the echoing castle walls, shouting, 'Help, Uncle Jim! Help!'

'You stop here,' said Potter to Johnson. They had no idea it was really Julian speaking. 'I'll go and see what's up.'

In his own turn, *he* ran to the doorway, and fell over the same piece of string. He wasn't as lucky as Gary, who was only stunned – he fell with one leg folded awkwardly under him.

'My leg!' he yelled. 'I think I've broken it!'

In the shadows, George smiled. She was pretty sure he had only sprained an ankle, but what a fuss he was making! 'Well, that's two of them out of action!' she whispered to her cousins and Tinker. 'Now for the third!'

'Woof!' barked Timmy, as if he were taking part in the conversation.

'Hear that?' said Dick. 'Sounds as if Timmy wants to join the fun!'

'Well, he certainly deserves to!' said George. 'I expect he'd like his revenge – go on, then, good dog! Get him!'

Timmy didn't need to be told twice. Before Johnson had time to come to Potter's aid, he found he was being attacked by a furious creature who rushed at him fangs bared!

'That dog!' he thought in amazement. 'So he didn't drown after all!'

And then his instinct for self-preservation sent him running away, as fast as he could.

'Now!' cried Julian. 'To the boat, everyone!'

George, Julian, Dick, Anne and Tinker ran down the path, carrying Mischief and the treasure, which they had taken out of the casket and wrapped carefully in pieces of blanket. They took great care not to step on the patches of oil, and jumped into the motor-boat. Then George whistled to Timmy, who stopped watching Johnson – the man had climbed a tree to get away from him – and ran to join the others.

Three minutes later the Mandevilles' motor-boat, carrying the happy children, was making for the mainland and Kirrin Cottage. Soon they could see the lights of the house itself.

'Uncle Quentin and Professor Hayling must be hard at work as usual!' said Julian. 'What a surprise they'll get! Hey, George – why are you changing course?'

'Er . . . well,' said George, 'I think the best thing to do is go to Kirrin village first and tell the police, like good citizens!'

Dick couldn't help laughing. 'I see!' he said. 'You think your father won't be so cross with us in front of a few policemen! I must admit we've run rather a lot of risks during this adventure – and Uncle Quentin *does* tend to lose his temper when we go running risks!'

The men on duty at Kirrin police station were very surprised when the children turned up, carrying the treasure, and told them what had been happening. They soon realised, however, that they would get lots of very good publicity in the newspapers if they arrested the men who had gone off with the Mandeville inheritance!

'I believe Mr Mandeville got home this very evening,' said the Sergeant. 'There were lights on in Wisteria Lodge when I was passing just now.'

Then a great many things happened all at once. Tinker telephoned Jenny, George telephoned her father, and the police telephoned the Mandevilles, while several men went off to get the police launch and go out to Kirrin Island to pick up the crooks. Mr and Mrs Mandeville were astonished to hear of all that had been happening while they were away in London, and Mr Mandeville came straight round to the police station.

'Has someone gone to arrest Johnson and his friends?' he asked. 'Good! A nice catch for you – and you'll owe it all to these children, you know! As for me, *I* owe them even more!' he added, smiling.

It certainly was a good catch that the policemen brought back from Kirrin Island! Johnson was furious and disappointed, Gary had a bump as big as a duck's egg on his forehead, and Potter was wailing and moaning that his leg was broken. Johnson and his nephew were taken off to prison, and Potter was sent to the hospital, under police escort. The Kirrin police had phoned Scotland Yard to tell them the name of the fence, Tracy, and he was being arrested too. He was already known to the London police force as a very shady character, and when they searched his flat they got all the proof they needed of what he did for a living.

Next day, Mr and Mrs Mandeville invited the children, their parents and Jenny to lunch at Wisteria Lodge. It was a very cheerful meal – though interrupted several times by radio reporters who had found out where the children were, and were calling to ask them to say a few words. They even asked Timmy to bark for the listeners, too! Mr Mandeville told George and the others that he was going to use part of the treasure to build a modern Children's Home in the country near Kirrin.

Mrs Mandeville said she thought the Five and Tinker ought to have a reward themselves – and she gave each of the children two of the gold coins from the treasure, dating back to the time of King Charles I. 'As a souvenir of your adventures!' she said, smiling.

George was very relieved that she hadn't been scolded by her father, and she was delighted with her two coins. 'Oh, thank you!' she said, and she added, with a mischievous smile, 'Actually, it was high time you and Mr Mandeville came home to take possession of Lady Mandeville's treasure. If you'd been away much longer, I've a feeling it might easily have vanished again. It's a kind of disappearing treasure – now you see it, now you don't! You'd better keep it well locked up, in case it gets away once more!'

And the festive meal ended in gales of laughter.

If you liked this book by Claude Voilier, you are certain to enjoy the original Famous Five stories by Enid Blyton. These are published by Hodder Children's Books: